NOV   2003

Love

in the

Shadows

Love
in the
Shadows

Joanne Lennox

THORNDIKE
CHIVERS

This Large Print edition is published by Thorndike Press®, Waterville, Maine USA and by BBC Audiobooks, Ltd, Bath, England.

Published in 2003 in the U.S. by arrangement with Dorian Literary Agency.

Published in 2003 in the U.K. by arrangement with the author.

U.S. Hardcover 0-7862-5927-2 (Candlelight)
U.K. Hardcover 0-7540-7724-1   (Chivers Large Print)

The text of this Large Print edition is unabridged.
Other aspects of the book may vary from the original edition.

Set in 16 pt. Plantin by Elena Picard.

Printed in the United States on permanent paper.

British Library Cataloguing-in-Publication Data available

Library of Congress Cataloging-in-Publication Data

Lennox, Joanne.
    Love in the shadows / Joanne Lennox.
        p. cm.
    ISBN 0-7862-5927-2 (lg. print : hc : alk. paper)
    1. England — Fiction. 2. Nannies — Fiction.
3. Social classes — Fiction. 4. Large type books. I. Title.
PR6062.E647L68 2003
    823′.92—dc22   2003058143

Love
in the
Shadows

Chapter One

"Would you mind telling me exactly what you think you're doing?" the question was fired at her in deep, curt tones, bringing Lauren back down to earth with an unpleasant bump.

She'd been mesmerised by the view from this vantage point — the lower land over towards Poole harbour, a patchwork of greens and yellows, where the sparkling sea was dotted with tiny islands and, on the skyline, the town itself, glowing in the sun. It was such a beautiful place, it was impossible to believe she had gone against her parents' wishes coming here.

Now Lauren spun round abruptly, to come face to face with the tall, darkly glowering owner of the curt voice.

"Well?" the man said and focused his dark gaze on Lauren, his well-spoken voice a fraction less threatening. "Are you going to tell me what you're doing up here?"

"What does it look like I'm doing?"

At over six feet, the man had a considerable height advantage over her five feet three inches, as well as possessing a powerful, muscular build, but Lauren tilted her chin up at him determinedly.

"I was taking a walk, admiring the view."

"That's all very well," the man replied, and this time Lauren noticed that his dark brown eyes were almost the colour of treacle, and that the cropped curls on the top of his head were tousled gently by the breeze, "except that you happen to be admiring my private view from my private land."

"Oh!" Lauren exclaimed, surprised.

The last time she had come up here, back in May, for the interview, she'd approached the house from the front, from the north side of Gorse Hill.

"I'm sorry, I didn't realise. I just followed the path up from the village."

"Well, just make sure you don't do it again."

Something in his tone rankled with Lauren, the way he had spoken of his private view, and she couldn't help adding, "Anyway, why should you hog this wonderful view all to yourself? The countryside

8

should be for everyone. No-one should own it."

The stranger laughed then, a dry, mirthless chuckle.

"Try to see it from my point of view. How would you like all and sundry walking round your back garden?" he demanded.

"Well," Lauren retorted briskly "we haven't all got the luxury of a three-acre back garden!"

"A townie. I might have known! People like you are always leaving their sandwich wrappers lying around up here, letting their mobile phones scare the sheep," he half-growled. "You lot are all the same!"

"Who are you calling a townie?" Lauren exclaimed indignantly.

Just because the settlement of Gorse Hill was small enough to qualify for village status, the fact that she herself came from the small, neighbouring town of Ecclesdon was neither here nor there.

"Or is that your term for anyone who hasn't got straw coming out of their ears?"

The man made no reply, simply deepened his glower still further.

"Anyway," Lauren surged on, "I'll have you know that my ancestors have lived round these parts for ages!"

"OK, so maybe that was a bit of a sweeping statement," he conceded grudgingly. "It's just that we get a lot of trouble with trespassers up here, and it's made me rather wary about allowing intruders on to my land."

"For goodness' sake!" she commented mildly. "What's there to be so secretive about? What are you hiding up here? A whisky distillery? Or maybe a secret casino?"

The man's eyes narrowed again as her barb hit home.

"Haven't you heard," he shot quickly back, "that sarcasm is the lowest form of wit?"

"At least I haven't had a sense-of-humour bypass," Lauren replied, tossing back her long, sunstreaked brown hair haughtily.

There was a pause, while Lauren braced herself for the next insulting reply. To her surprise, however, the man replied, "Touché," with an inclination of his head, and what was almost a smile. There was another pause. Then, tentatively, Lauren smiled back. For a moment it almost seemed they had reached a truce. Then, ever-practical, Lauren felt compelled to add, "But anyway, shouldn't you have a gate if you're that bothered about trespassers?"

"I have got a gate, as a matter of fact," the dark stranger replied, his tone becoming more abrupt once again "and you must have had your eyes closed when you strolled through it a couple of minutes ago."

Indignance rising once more, Lauren retorted, "Well, there's not much point having a gate if you can't even be bothered to keep it closed. It's practically inviting riff-raff like me on to your property," she added, her green eyes glowing mischievously. "And you hear so much about burglaries these days."

"Quite," the man replied.

If he appreciated her attempt at humour, he didn't show it. In fact, if anything, his mouth seemed to tighten still further, as if she had made a tasteless remark.

"And now, I'm sorry to curtail our cosy little chat but I've got things to attend to."

About to walk off, he turned back at the last minute.

"Oh, and would you mind closing the gate behind you on your way out?"

"Yes, sir."

With an exaggerated show of humility, Lauren tugged an imaginary forelock.

"And I promise not to stray on to your

manor again, your lordship."

"Just see that you don't."

It was hard to gauge whether the man was joking or not. Then he was gone, striding off across the heathland, presumably in the direction of his mansion. For a few moments Lauren stood staring after him, thinking what an arrogant, objectionable man she had just had the misfortune to bump into. What a shame, she added bitterly to herself, that he was about to become her new neighbour!

Then she gathered her thoughts together and set off back in the direction of the path. When, in due course, she came to the man's white-painted gate she slammed it behind her with slightly more force than was strictly necessary, noting it was numbered twelve.

Realising that she must have missed number ten, Lauren retraced her steps a few hundred yards down the hill. The next gate Lauren came to indeed proclaimed itself to belong to a property numbered ten and called Misty Towers and, unlike its neighbour, this gate was firmly and sensibly closed. A light mist was indeed descending, as Lauren followed a path through the sizeable back garden. After walking a hundred yards or so, she saw that the grass

12

was cropped and neater, and the flowers and plants were more strictly regimented into beds. Then suddenly the house itself appeared out of the descending mist, a large building of grey stone, flanked by the twin, turreted towers which gave it its unusual name.

"Misty Towers. Typical Victorian sense of melodrama," Geoffrey Ferguson had said on their first meeting, but Lauren had rather liked the name.

The house looked different from the rear, Lauren thought, more forbidding. In spite of herself, in spite of the welcoming lights flickering at the leaded windows, and the roses and ivy that climbed the walls, Lauren found herself remembering her parents' warning.

"No good ever came to our family from the folk of Gorse Hill," her mother had said mysteriously, her father shaking his head in agreement in the background.

Lauren had pressed both parents for more information, but none had been forthcoming. Remembering this now, she gave an involuntary shiver.

Half an hour or so later, Lauren's spirits had rallied, as she found herself back in the Fergusons' spacious sitting-room. She had been plied with tea and delicious cake, and was surrounded by friendly, welcoming faces.

"Now then, Lauren."

Geoffrey Ferguson was a pleasant, robust-looking man in his forties, with silver hair and amiable blue-grey eyes. At her interview he'd told her that he used to work for a merchant bank in the city, but was now semi-retired and worked from home as an investment consultant.

Her new employer now continued, "Let me introduce you to the rest of the family. You've met my wife, Christine."

"Hello, again, Lauren."

"Hello, Christine. How are you?"

Lauren exchanged greetings with a handsome woman in her early forties, her greying auburn hair swept up into a chignon, striking blue eyes smiling back at Lauren. Christine was, Lauren believed, what was known as a "lady who lunched."

"I'm fine, thanks, Lauren. Recovering from the shock . . ." then as if remembering herself, Christine broke off suddenly. "Of course, you don't know there's been a bit of a to-do since you were last here."

To Lauren's bemusement, Geoffrey shot his wife a warning glance.

"We'll come to that later. Anyway,

Lauren, I don't believe you've met our daughter, Jane, or Janey, as she's more commonly known."

So this was the Fergusons' eighteen-year-old daughter, Lauren observed.

"Our first-born," Geoffrey continued, confirming her thoughts, "and very proud we are of her, too."

"Daddy," Janey groaned, embarrassed by the show of emotion.

Then she turned apologetically to Lauren.

"Hi," she said wryly.

Lauren smiled warmly back at Janey, a pretty, slender young woman with her mother's auburn hair, cut into a fashionable crop.

"And, of course, this young man," Geoffrey was concluding, before Lauren had time to collect her thoughts, "is the main reason you're here. Come and say hello to Lauren, Daniel. You'll have your hands full looking after him," he added with a wink.

And so Lauren fixed her gaze, for the second time, on two-year-old Daniel Ferguson, the little boy whose nanny she was to become. Almost inevitably, he had his sister's and mother's auburn hair and wide, cat-like eyes, but in his case they were set in an impudent, pixie-face, accentuated by a cute, pointed chin. It was clear the two Ferguson children took after their mother in their colouring, while they appeared to have inherited their father's height.

"Hello, Daniel," Lauren said, her voice soft and unthreatening. "You remember me, don't you? I'm going to help your mummy and daddy look after you."

Daniel, who had been sitting between his parents on the chintz-covered settee, grinned and turned away, burying his head in the side of his mother's cashmere sweater.

"He's a bit shy," Christine apologised, "until he gets to know people."

"They all are at that age, aren't they?" Lauren agreed sympathetically, recalling her experiences with young children while studying for her diploma, and also with her twin younger brothers, Michael and Christopher. "I'm sure we'll soon get to know each other, won't we, Daniel?"

She was rewarded by the little boy extracting his head from his mother's side, and flashing a cheeky smile at her. Geoffrey cleared his throat.

"Anyway, as my wife mentioned earlier, there was a bit of a commotion after we saw you last. You see, the following week, it was discovered that something had gone missing from the house. Oh, nothing big," he went on, seeing Lauren's shocked expression "just a silver card case, but it was mid-nineteenth century, and worth about three hundred pounds. But, as Christine said, it isn't so much the money, more the thought that there is a thief in our midst."

"Oh, how awful," Lauren breathed.

"It was awful," Christine agreed, "especially at first. I couldn't help looking at everyone in the house through new, suspicious eyes."

Lauren clasped a hand to her mouth in sudden, horrified realisation.

"Of course. It happened about a week after I had been here. You must have suspected me, too."

"Well, no more than anyone else."

"You know how it is," but both Geoffrey and Christine seemed to shift awkwardly on the sofa.

"Mr and Mrs Ferguson," Lauren began earnestly, "I swear I have never stolen from anyone in my life, and would certainly never contemplate stealing from my new employers."

"Well, that was what we hoped," Christine said, to Lauren's great relief. "And we checked your references, and they seemed to be exemplary."

17

"And Christine was keen to give you a chance," Geoffrey finished. "So I agreed."

"It's so hard to get good staff these days," Christine added. "And Daniel seemed fond of you."

"Thank you both for giving me a chance," Lauren said gratefully. "I swear I won't let you down. So you still don't know who the thief was?"

"No," Geoffrey replied briskly. "And I don't suppose we ever will. There was no sign of a forced entry, but regrettably we'd left a small window open in the sitting-room that night. There were no finger-prints at the scene. Probably some passing opportunist."

"Yes, how awful," Lauren said. "Still," she continued, marginally more brightly, "let's just hope it doesn't happen again."

"Quite," Geoffrey and Christine both agreed. "The police advised us to install a burglar alarm," Christine went on, "which we've done. It should be a deterrent, should anyone try to chance his luck again."

At that point there was a knock at the sitting-room door.

"Come in," Geoffrey called casually, and a middle-aged couple entered. "Come and meet Lauren James, our new nanny,"

Geoffrey Ferguson continued, as the couple crossed the polished, wooden floor, with its scattering of expensive-looking Persian rugs. "Maggie Foster, our very talented cook," Geoffrey told Lauren. "And her husband, Derek, our, er . . ."

"Odd-job man?" Derek offered, with a smile.

"Chauffeur and gardener, I was going to say," Geoffrey supplied quickly.

Lauren smiled at the couple, aware that they, too, would be under suspicion.

"Delighted to meet you both," Lauren said, wondering how she was ever going to remember so many new names and faces.

Maggie Foster strained her ears.

"That's the doorbell. Do excuse me, Lauren, I'll just go and answer it," and she bustled away.

"Tea, cake, Derek?" Christine Ferguson offered, and Lauren turned her attention back to Daniel, who was now perching on the edge of the settee, staring curiously at her.

Then the little boy hopped down on to the floor and retrieved a small toy car, which he presented to Lauren.

"Oh, thank you, Daniel!"

Lauren kneeled down beside him, encouraged. She had learned that the best way with children was to leave them until they chose to approach.

"That's a lovely car. Is it yours?"

"Yes," Daniel offered with a shy grin. "S'mine, that car." Then Lauren heard footsteps re-entering the room and Maggie Foster's voice saying, "Mr Rossiter to see you, Mr Ferguson."

"Ah, excellent," Geoffrey replied. "Hello, Jake. This is Lauren, our new nanny. Good chance for you to meet the neighbour, too, Lauren."

Feeling rather at a disadvantage from her position crouched on the floor beside Daniel, Lauren twisted her head round and looked up. A tall man towered above her, but because the light from the picture window was behind him his face and figure were shadowy. Trying to hide her awkwardness, Lauren said the first thing that came into her head.

"Jake? I always think of that as being a pirate's name."

There was general laughter from the gathered group, but the moment Lauren had spoken she could have kicked herself. She hardly heard Geoffrey's introduction as the tall stranger extended his hand in greeting. Scrambling to her feet, Lauren took the hand, whose grip was firm.

"A pirate, eh, Miss James — Lauren?" the man said mockingly. "On the contrary, I think you'll find it's not me, but you who's the lawbreaker."

Lauren's brow furrowed and, in spite of herself, her heart started to pound. Talk of the burglary was all too fresh in her ears.

"What do you mean, Mr Rossiter?"

Jake Rossiter shifted slightly, and suddenly his face was visible to Lauren and she realised her terrible faux-pas.

"So short a memory, Lauren? Why, it can scarcely be forty-five minutes since I caught you trespassing in my garden!"

A stunned hush fell on the assembled group, and Lauren felt her cheeks flaming as all eyes suddenly seemed to focus on her. Then Geoffrey Ferguson broke the silence with a hearty laugh.

"What's this, Lauren? You've only been here a few minutes and already you're getting on the wrong side of the neighbours! It won't do, you know!"

Full of shame and embarrassment, and wanting to kick Jake Rossiter for his ill-chosen, smart remark, Lauren said through gritted teeth, "I wasn't aware at the time that I was trespassing, Mr Ferguson, and I've already apologised to Mr Rossiter for my mistake."

"It's quite all right, Lauren," Geoffrey Ferguson said heartily. "I don't think any further apologies will be necessary. I'm sure Jake was joking. You'll soon get used to his warped sense of humour. No, seriously, Lauren, Jake's a perfect gentleman, and one of my oldest and closest friends."

Lauren thought privately that she would have expected Geoffrey Ferguson to have better taste than that, but she kept the thought to herself.

"I advise Jake on financial matters," Geoffrey was going on. "And he gives me the benefit of his antiques expertise."

"Would you like some tea, Mr Rossiter?" Maggie Foster was offering.

"Please, Maggie," Jake replied, in that smooth, deep voice of his.

Lauren gazed warily at him, trying to estimate his age. Late thirties, she guessed. Not that she cared, anyway.

The gentle hum of conversation seemed to have started up again. Lauren looked about for Daniel but to her disappointment the little boy had scrambled back on to his mother's knee, leaving her no choice but to make conversation with the objectionable Jake Rossiter.

"So, Mr Rossiter," Lauren asked politely, "what do you do for a living?"

"There's no need for such formality," the man protested. "If we are to be neighbours, Lauren, we might as well be on first-name terms."

Jake turned his eyes on her, and Lauren found to her surprise that her heart, normally perfectly reliable in its steadiness, started to pound again.

"OK," she said, annoyed at how unsteady her voice sounded, "Jake."

"Well," Jake went on, "contrary to your beliefs, Lauren, there's not much call for piracy round here these days. No, instead I opted for the marginally less incriminating vocation of antiques dealer."

"Oh, yes?" Lauren asked.

Suddenly she thought of the stolen silver card case, and was unable to prevent a suspicion from hovering in her mind. Her wariness deepened and she couldn't help saying, "I've heard they can be dubious characters, too."

Recalling a television documentary she had seen, Lauren went on, "Going round to the houses of vulnerable, old ladies, offering to take some valuable antique off their hands for a fraction of its value."

A trace of annoyance crossed Jake's ruggedly handsome features.

"I'm not a knocker, Lauren, if that's

what you're implying. I think those sorts of people are as despicable as you clearly do."

For a moment his denial left Lauren wrong-footed, then she answered with faultless logic, "Well, you're bound to deny it, aren't you? Those people thrive on presenting a respectable image to the world, when all the while . . ."

An electronic beeping emanated from Jake's jacket pocket.

"Excuse me a moment," he muttered irritably, and produced a mobile phone. "Hello?" he barked, and then proceeded to conduct a conversation under his breath while Lauren stood awkwardly beside him.

Lauren was filled with fresh indignation. Was this the man who, less than an hour earlier, had been slandering so-called townies and their mobile phones? Why, this man was not only rude, he was hypocritical, too! A couple of minutes later he switched off the phone and slipped it back into his pocket.

"Again, my apologies, Lauren. Something's come up, business," he clarified, as if Lauren cared less whether it was business or personal. "Make my excuses to Geoff, would you?"

He gestured towards their host, who was on the other side of the room, engrossed in conversation with Derek Foster. Lauren was almost speechless at this man's arrogance and lack of consideration.

"Couldn't you spare a minute to say goodbye to him yourself? After all," she challenged, "he is your closest friend."

"That's why he'll understand," Jake grated, sounding more curt and impatient than ever. "Especially if you tell him it's business."

And with that he was gone, leaving Lauren staring after him. Once again she was breathlessly indignant, and yet somehow strangely shaken.

Chapter Two

That evening Lauren sat on the bed in her new room, gazing into the mirror on her tiny dressing-table. An hour ago she had used the Ferguson family phone to ring her mother, who had been delighted to hear from her only daughter, if unable to disguise her lingering reservations about Lauren's new job.

"I just think you could set your sights higher than being a nanny, darling," Carole James had sighed. "You're such a clever girl, I'm sure you could be a primary teacher, if you wanted to."

"But, Mum, being a nanny is a worthwhile and rewarding job!" Lauren had retorted exasperatedly, having been over this ground many times in the past few days. "And besides, it's exactly what I want to do."

"If you say so, Lauren," her mother's voice had softened. "But I worry about you, away from home, with strange people, and in Gorse Hill."

At this point Lauren had recalled the burglary. There was no way she could mention it to her mother, or she would have a sleepless night worrying about it. So instead, Lauren had laughed. She lowered her voice in case someone walked into the sitting-room, where she was phoning.

"There's nothing strange about the Fergusons, Mum. They're really nice people, and I'm a big girl now."

"I know, darling, but I can't help worrying. I've never told you this before, but your great-grandma, my mother's mother, once worked in a house in Gorse Hill, a big house, like the one you're in. She was a housemaid."

"Really?" Lauren asked. "Why didn't you mention this till now?"

"I hoped it wouldn't be necessary to dredge up the unpleasant details. Best to let sleeping dogs lie. Even now, the family finds the whole business rather distressing. Suffice it to say," she went on, having regained her composure "that your great-grandmother was not well-treated by her employers."

There was an awkward silence. Not only was her mother still keeping part of the

27

truth from her, but she in return wasn't telling her mother about the stolen card case. Uneasily, Lauren reassured the older woman.

"I must go now. Promise not to worry, Mum, and give my love to Dad."

Now, having helped Christine bath and put Daniel to bed in his room across the passageway from her, Lauren was preparing for dinner with the Fergusons. As it was her first night, she was to dine with the family. She had been forewarned that the Fergusons' vet, Stephen Hughes, was also attending the dinner.

"You must meet Stephen, Lauren," Janey had told her. "He's really dishy and," she continued, mindful of her father's watchful gaze, "single! You never know," she continued eagerly, "you two might hit it off."

At the time, Lauren had made light of Janey's provocative comment. Now, though, she couldn't help being just slightly intrigued to meet this handsome, eligible man who was to join them for dinner. She had put on the one decent dress she'd brought, a sleeveless cornflower blue shift. Most of her wardrobe consisted of practical, sensible clothes, but on a shopping trip with her friend, Sally, she'd been persuaded to buy this luxurious item.

"Oh, you've simply got to have it, Laurie," Sally had urged. "It looks gorgeous with your eyes, and sets your hair off a treat."

Satisfied that she was as presentable as she was ever going to be, Lauren closed the door of her little room behind her and stepped into the rather gloomy passage. It was an old house, mid-Victorian, Geoffrey Ferguson had told her and her bedroom, near the nursery, had once belonged to the governess. For a moment, as she descended the small, spiral staircase that led to the sitting-room, Lauren felt a pang of empathy with that long-ago servant, probably a young woman away from home for the first time like herself, like her great-grandmother, she wondered.

"Lauren, you look simply lovely, my dear!" Christine Ferguson greeted her as she entered the sitting-room.

"Er — thank you, Mrs Ferguson."

Lauren felt nervous and slightly daunted, seeing the rest of the family already assembled at the far end of the sitting-room, enjoying pre-dinner drinks, together with a slim, fair man in his late twenties who must be Stephen Hughes.

A pleased-looking Janey came over to her, dragging him by the arm.

"Lauren, this is Stephen. You know, the one I was telling you about?"

"Oh, yes," Lauren murmured, feeling the blush rising to her cheeks and hoping it wasn't patently obvious to Stephen what Janey had been saying. "The family vet."

Lauren tried to sound as businesslike as possible. Stephen Hughes extended his hand, which she took.

"Something like that, yes. I take care of the Fergusons' many horses. Christine and Geoffrey used to be passionate about Labradors, too, but unfortunately they're unable to own a dog now due to little Daniel's allergy."

"Ah, yes," Lauren said, remembering. "Mr Ferguson mentioned that at the interview."

"Anyway, as I said, I look after the family's horses, have done for almost a year now, although I also like to think of myself as a family friend."

"Stephen, how dare you presume such a thing?" Janey teased.

Stephen cuffed her playfully around the head.

"Well, if these roughnecks won't be civil, perhaps you would do me the honour of being my friend, Lauren?"

Stephen Hughes' dark blue eyes gazed

expectantly at her. Lauren was instantly won over.

"Of course I'll be your friend, Stephen," she said, inclining her head.

The moment was broken by the arrival of Maggie Foster to say that dinner was served.

The group moved up to take their places at the long mahogany dining-table at the other end of the vast room. Lauren found herself next to Stephen to her left and an empty chair to her right. A nasty suspicion was beginning to form in her mind when the door at the far end of the room opened again and her fears were confirmed.

"Ah, Jake!"

Geoffrey rose from his chair to greet his friend.

"Glad you could join us!"

Jake Rossiter, on his way to the table, suddenly seemed to notice Lauren. As if he was surprised to see her there, Lauren felt him hold her gaze. She was unable to look away, till he did so first.

"My deepest apologies for being late," Jake Rossiter said smoothly to the party in general. "A matter of business, I'm afraid. Something cropped up that just couldn't wait."

To Lauren it seemed that Jake Rossiter

had a habit of putting business before friendship, and her instinctive dislike for him deepened. As he went to take his place beside her, however, she couldn't help noticing that his casual attire of that afternoon had been replaced by a dark, expensive-looking suit, teamed with a silver-grey shirt and matching tie. Even his unruly hair had been tamed with a touch of gel. Her heart skipped an involuntary beat. He really was a devastatingly good-looking man. If only her friend, Sally, could see her now, Lauren thought with a wry grin, seated between two such handsome men.

Lauren was suddenly aware that Jake was speaking to her.

"You will forgive me, won't you, Lauren, for the appalling manners I've displayed yet again?"

Caught off-guard, she replied, "Um — of course," having the sneaking feeling that he was mocking her, so she asked flippantly, "What's there to forgive?"

"That's very decent of you. And might I add," Jake went on smoothly, his eyes flickering over her, "that you are looking very nice tonight."

Then his treacle-dark eyes met hers again. When at last Lauren was able to look away, she found her heart was pounding wildly.

"So, Jake," Geoffrey asked across the table, as Maggie served them all with carrot and coriander soup, "how is business? Any interesting pieces crop up lately?"

At this, Lauren was all ears.

"Funny you should say that," Jake replied. "I came across a rather nice maple desk and bookcase yesterday, Rhode Island Chippendale."

"Really?" Geoffrey asked keenly, trying, Lauren guessed, to sound more knowledgeable than he actually was, although, looking around, it was clear that Geoffrey was the proud owner of several valuable antiques himself. "I don't know, Jake," Geoffrey went on jokily. "You have all the luck. Funny how the best pieces always seem to fall into your lap!"

Such as an eighteenth-century card case, Lauren wondered suddenly.

"Yes, and I picked it up for a song, too!" Jake added, with a sideways wink at Lauren.

Startled, she was once again unsure whether the man was joking or not.

"Yes, well I expect old ladies are a pushover once you've got them feeling flustered and under pressure," she flung at him defensively.

There was a ripple of nervous, uncertain laughter from around the table, as Lauren realised the whole party was mesmerised by the conversation, her other neighbour, the dashing Stephen Hughes, included. Jake, too, was regarding her steadily.

"Yes, you're right, Lauren, I did buy the piece from an old lady, but I think you underestimate the elderly. This particular woman was not only charming but as sharp as a knife, and I can assure you she got a good price for her treasured possession."

This left Lauren at a momentary loss for words.

"I'm glad to hear it," she eventually muttered, though, privately, she was loath to believe a word of it.

As she spoke, she sensed relief from around the table.

Jake was looking at Lauren challengingly.

"I don't know. What do you say, Lauren?" His dark, humorous eyes seemed to mock her. "Truce?"

With everyone's eyes upon her, Lauren could see no way out of it.

"Truce," she agreed, grudgingly.

Lauren turned away. She was getting fed up of Jake Rossiter's smooth-talking, and the fact that, although he had plenty to say for himself, he never actually gave any personal information away.

When they eventually finished dessert and adjourned to the other end of the room to drink their coffee in comfort, Lauren was relieved to be joined on the sofa not by Jake, but by Stephen Hughes. Jake himself, Lauren noticed, was standing nearby, uncharacteristically quiet. He stared broodingly out of the picture window, his tall figure hovering on the edge of her vision like a persistent black thundercloud.

"So, you're the Fergusons' new nanny," Stephen began. "But do I detect, from your accent, that you're not entirely new to the area?"

"That's right," Lauren confirmed, flattered that Stephen had noticed. "I come from Ecclesdon actually, just down the road. What about yourself? I'm no expert, but is that a London accent I can hear?"

"Got it in one," Stephen agreed. "You're good at this. You should turn professional."

"I think I'll stick to nannying, thank you," Lauren replied, laughing.

Out of the corner of her eye, she was

sure Jake was glaring at her.

"So," she persisted, ignoring Jake, "what made you move to the area?"

Stephen's smile died at this, and he lowered his voice confidentially.

"To be honest, it was a difficult time in my life, and I just wanted to get away from it all."

He gave what seemed to Lauren a wary glance at Geoffrey Ferguson, who had come over to talk to Jake. Lauren thought she caught the phrase, three thousand pounds. The men seemed to be discussing an ornately-painted vase that stood on a small, antique-looking table, near the window.

"My marriage had broken up, you see, and I fancied a complete change," Stephen was continuing. "I'd always admired the scenery of the West Country. I'm mad about sailing, too, which there's plenty of round here. So I came to live here."

"Oh, right."

Setting her cup in its saucer with a loud chink, Lauren fought to disguise her surprise at this revelation. Stephen seemed to sense her feelings.

"I've shocked you," he said quietly, his dark blue eyes concerned. "Of course, I'm not proud that my marriage didn't work out, but the split between Wendy and me was amicable, and thank goodness, there were no children involved."

"I'm sorry."

Lauren gathered her wits together.

"You must think I'm so rude. I didn't mean to gawp at you. It's just that you don't seem that much older than me," she admitted, opting for honesty. "I would never have guessed you'd been married once already."

"Well, there it is," Stephen shrugged. "It's out in the open now. So what do you say. Do you still want to be my friend?"

Lauren couldn't help laughing at this.

"Don't be silly, Stephen, of course I'll still be your friend."

"Great! Well, then, let's drink to a long and beautiful friendship." Stephen raised his coffee cup and chinked it against hers.

"To a long and beautiful friendship," she echoed.

Her smile faded as she noticed Jake had finished his conversation with Geoffrey and was coming over to them.

"Is this a private toast," his deep, smooth voice broke in, "or can anyone join in?"

Stephen grinned conspiratorially at Lauren.

"Lauren and I were just toasting our

friendship," he told Jake.

Was it Lauren's imagination, or was the younger man's tone deliberately provocative?

"Oh, really?"

Jake raised an ironic eyebrow in response.

"I was about to tell Lauren that, if she plays her cards right," Stephen went on, looking not at Jake but straight at her, "I might even take her out on my yacht one day."

"Your yacht?" Lauren said incredulously.

"Yes, a yacht?" Jake Rossiter echoed, his tone deeply sceptical. "I didn't know you'd won the lottery, Stephen."

Stephen raised a blond eyebrow at Jake.

"I don't even do the lottery, but it's amazing what you can achieve if you save hard enough. I had a small legacy left to me by my late grandfather, too. Needless to say, I cleaned out my building society account when I bought it."

"I should think so," Jake was going on. "Some of those yachts set you back tens of thousands of pounds."

"It's only a modest one," Stephen said quickly. "Not one of those huge affairs you see over in Poole harbour."

"But still," Lauren added, with a glance

at Jake, "a yacht. I'm impressed."

Stephen shrugged.

"I said I was mad about sailing. So, Lauren, promise me you'll come out on the boat with me one day."

"Promise," Lauren agreed gladly.

At this point, an eager-looking Janey Ferguson materialised from nowhere, her green eyes alight with devilment, cheeks flushed with unaccustomed alcohol.

"What's this about sailing, Stephen? I'm always angling for an invitation to come out on your yacht, and you never offer to take me."

"Haven't you heard that patience is a virtue, missy?" Stephen told Janey with an avuncular smile. "Maybe when you're a bit older I'll take you out."

"Are you sure it's a yacht, and not just one of those smaller dinghies, Stephen?" Jake persisted, his tone dry and mocking.

Lauren glared at Jake, wishing he would stop being so rude and give poor Stephen a break.

"Don't listen to him," she assured Stephen. "I expect he's just jealous."

"Yes," Jake replied sarcastically, "I'm mad with envy at the thought of being tossed about in a small boat on ten-foot waves."

Once again he glanced at his wristwatch.

"And now, my deepest apologies to the three of you, but I'm afraid I must be going."

Janey and Stephen said their goodbyes, and promptly fell into a discussion about Janey's horse, Saladin, which just left Lauren and Jake.

"Surely not more business?" Lauren asked. "At this time of night?"

By her own reckoning, it was gone nine o'clock.

"Not tonight, no," Jake confirmed. "But I've got an antiques fair to go to tomorrow morning, the other side of Dorchester. And you know what they say about early birds catching worms."

Lauren supposed she did, but the only worm she could think of right then was standing before her, about six foot two in height, dark haired and with roguish dark eyes.

"Good-night, Chrissie, Geoff," Jake called across the room. "My deepest thanks for a most entertaining evening."

" 'Night, Jake," the couple called out in unison, from where they were comfortably ensconced on the other sofa.

"Don't bother getting up," Jake called back, taking Lauren's arm. "Lauren will see me out."

"I will do nothing of the sort," Lauren muttered indignantly, snatching her arm away.

"Oh, but I think you will," Jake whispered, his mouth close to her ear.

Suddenly Lauren was uncomfortably aware of his maleness, and his undeniable attractiveness.

"Remember, as of tomorrow, you're officially the Fergusons' employee, and think how it would repay their hospitality if you refused to perform this small service now."

Her heart pounding, Lauren could think of no answer to this, so she just glowered at him. Her eyes smouldered fire as the two of them walked towards the opened French windows, Jake having taken her arm once again. They stepped out into the long back garden, the July evening still warm and only just beginning to darken. The air around them was fragrant with the heady scent of rhododendrons. They walked until they were just out of sight of the sitting-room and then Jake stopped.

"I must thank you for this evening," he said and suddenly his voice was low and uncharacteristically serious. "I meant it when I told Geoff and Chrissie it had been enjoyable, and I have to admit that it was chiefly so because of your company."

41

For a moment Lauren was stunned, lost for words as she stared, face to face with Jake Rossiter, mesmerised by his dark eyes. Then her natural level-headedness returned.

"Oh, hang on, for a second there you almost had me! I almost forgot that charming people is what you do for a living!"

"Maybe," Jake said with a shrug. "But I meant what I just said."

Lauren frowned, a gentle sea breeze lifting her golden-brown hair.

"But I don't understand. Ever since we met, we've done nothing but argue."

The corners of Jake's mouth lifted with amusement.

"But it's been fun, hasn't it?"

For a second Lauren was almost tempted to agree with him. Fortunately she managed to compromise with a non-committal, "I don't know."

But Jake was staring intently at her now, gently taking each of her wrists in his large, sensual hands. Lauren found herself making no move to pull away and, as their eyes remained locked, she felt the electricity crackle between them. She was sure he was going to kiss her, and not at all sure that she minded. Then, to her disappointment, he released her.

"Good-night, Lauren," he said quietly. "Thank Geoff and Chrissie again, would you, for a very pleasant evening?"

Finally Lauren got a grip on herself. How could she have almost let this man kiss her?

"No, I won't be your messenger, Mr Rossiter," she called to his retreating figure. "I'm the Fergusons' nanny, not your slave."

"Fair enough," Jake called back equably, starting to make his way down the garden towards the distant cliff-top.

That night, an exhausted Lauren slept soundly, but her dreams were troubled by missing antiques and dark strangers. Around her, the unfamiliar house creaked and groaned in the restless sea wind, occasionally breaking through into her nocturnal reveries.

It was something of a relief to be woken at six by her alarm clock. Lauren dressed in a slim, neat skirt and fitted top, and was ready for Daniel when he woke at half past. She was immensely gratified when the little boy climbed out of bed on to her lap, and flung his arms around her.

Some time later they were eating breakfast in the large, oak-furnished kitchen, accompanied by the background burble of the radio, and the amiable housekeeper, Maggie, who seemed to know all Daniel's habits.

"Want juice," Daniel said shyly, once Lauren had sat him at the table.

"OK, just a minute," Lauren told him with a smile. "I'll get you some."

"I wouldn't if I were you," Maggie advised, as she spooned coffee into a percolator. "Did he have milk first thing?"

Lauren nodded, having been told by Christine that Daniel liked to wake with a bottle of milk.

"In that case, I should get something solid inside him first, if you want his breakfast to stay down."

"Sounds like you're the expert," Lauren said with a grin.

"I should be," Maggie replied. "I've had three of my own to practice on."

So, smiling, Lauren busied herself getting Daniel a bowl of cereal. As the room filled with the fragrant smell of coffee, the two-year-old rapidly seemed to be overcoming his shyness.

Before Lauren had a chance to start feeding him the cereal, he was impatiently chanting, "Want breakfast! Want breakfast!"

"Wait a minute, Daniel," Lauren said, her natural calm marginally threatened.

"It's just coming." Jokingly she added to Maggie, "I think I preferred him meek and mild."

Maggie was chuckling softly when the kitchen door was flung open and the cosy scene disrupted by a distressed-looking Christine Ferguson.

"Mummy!" Daniel cried eagerly, spraying a mouthful of cereal and milk on to his bib.

" 'Morning, darling, ladies," Christine murmured distractedly. "You wouldn't believe it, it really is too awful," she began disjointedly to the two women. "Geoffrey's in his study, phoning the police. You see, the green Coalport vase is missing. There's definitely a thief about, and it would appear that he's just struck again!"

"There, there," Maggie murmured soothingly to Christine a couple of minutes later, pressing her gently into a chair. "Sit down. You're probably in shock. Do you mind me asking," Maggie then asked discreetly, "how much the vase was worth?"

"About three thousand pounds."

Lauren gasped. Christine shook her head despairingly.

"I can't believe it's happened, again, only this time, the thief broke one of the small windows to get in."

"But what about the burglar alarm?" Lauren couldn't help asking. "Didn't it go off?"

"Geoffrey forgot to set it last night. He's in a terrible state about it, but what with the dinner and everything, we'd both had more than usual to drink."

"Easy enough to do," Maggie said understandingly.

"The police will have to interview everyone, of course," Christine added, glancing first at Maggie, then at Lauren, "and search their rooms."

"Of course."

Lauren swallowed uneasily, realising that, at the moment, she was probably top of the suspect list. Meanwhile, she was unable to rid herself of an image of Jake Rossiter standing with Geoffrey only last night, gazing down at a tall, elegant dark-green and gilt vase, decorated with paintings of exotic, colourful birds. He certainly knew about the value of antiques, and, being Geoffrey Ferguson's best friend, had the added advantage of being above suspicion.

The doorbell rang.

"That'll be the police," Christine said, as Maggie rushed to answer it.

Maggie returned, however, not with a

policeman but with Jake Rossiter. Lauren felt her heart beat faster at the sight of him. Could the man who'd almost kissed her last night be a criminal?

"Come in, Mr Rossiter," Maggie was saying. "I'll get you a cup of coffee."

" 'Morning, Jake," Christine murmured. "Isn't it too awful? Excuse me, I must see how Geoffrey's getting on."

She hurried out of the room. While Maggie busied herself with the coffee, Jake sat at the kitchen table with Lauren and Daniel.

" 'Morning, all."

"What are you doing here?" Lauren's hostility was thinly veiled as she spooned the last of Daniel's cereal deftly into his mouth. "I thought you had an antiques fair to go to."

"I do," Jake said briskly, "but Geoff phoned and told me the bad news and I promised I'd come over. And I suppose," he mused, "the police will want to interview me, as I was here last night."

"Yes, no-one's above suspicion," Lauren commented.

Their eyes met, and that familiar spark shot between them.

"Of course, that's how it should be," Jake agreed, perfectly composed. "I expect they'll want to speak to Stephen, too, seeing as he was here as well."

"Stephen!" Lauren exclaimed, shocked. "But I'm sure he wouldn't commit a terrible crime like that."

"No, but as you said," Jake said pointedly, "no-one's above suspicion. Actually, Geoff told me he was going to phone Stephen and tell him the bad news, get him to call in today."

"Want juice! Want juice!" Daniel interjected and Lauren rose to fetch him some from the fridge.

"Some might think that the criminal would be reluctant to return to the scene of the crime, so soon afterwards," she continued, gently but persistently probing.

"Indeed," Jake agreed. "Thanks, Maggie, you're an angel," he murmured, accepting his cup of coffee. "Although, some might also think that returning to the scene of the crime was a double bluff, by a criminal keen to give an impression of his — or her — innocence."

It was no longer clear whether they were talking about Jake, or Stephen or Lauren herself. Instantly, Lauren was on her guard.

"Why the emphasis on the feminine connection? Are you trying to imply that the burglar was a woman?"

Jake's treacle-brown eyes seemed to darken.

"Quite the contrary," he said crisply. "I am merely trying to keep an open mind. Although," he added with a glance at her, as if he'd guessed Lauren's suspicions, "I'm not so sure the same could be said of you."

Unaware of the hostile undercurrents, Daniel handed Lauren his beaker.

"All gone."

"Good boy."

Lauren wiped Daniel's face with a quick, neat movement.

"What do you mean, the same can't be said of me?" she challenged Jake, flushing under his intense scrutiny.

"Nothing." Jake shrugged, draining his coffee cup. "Just that you already appear to have formed certain suspicions of your own."

"Ah, Jake, Christine said you were here!"

A harassed Geoffrey rushed in.

"Shall we talk in the study? Maggie, would you bring coffee and toast through, and show the police officers through when they arrive?"

"Certainly," Maggie nodded, busying herself again at the other end of the kitchen.

Geoffrey rushed off and Jake got up to leave.

" 'Morning, everybody."

A subdued Stephen Hughes popped his head around the kitchen door, his hair slightly dishevelled, his mouth twisted. "Terrible news, isn't it?"

"Hello, Stephen," Jake greeted him. "Good grief, this is getting more like a French farce every minute, with all these comings and goings."

"Maybe it's more like a tragedy?" Lauren suggested, with a conspiratorial look at Stephen.

"Sadly, yes," Stephen agreed.

Lauren was aware of Jake glowering in the background. He attempted a smile.

"It's good to see you again, Lauren. I won't forget about that boating trip I promised you, although maybe we should postpone it to a happier time."

"Thank goodness for that," Jake said dryly. "I was about to have to ask Maggie to pass me the sick-bucket. Anyway, I won't play gooseberry any longer. I was just on my way to see Geoff. 'Bye, Lauren," Jake said to her, "and I'll warn you," he added, brown eyes narrowed as he alluded to their previous conversation, "not to go playing the amateur detective and jumping to conclusions about people. It'll do neither you nor anyone else any good."

For a moment Lauren was speechless.

"How dare you threaten me," she fumed then, her voice an indignant squeak.

But it was too late — Jake had already left and her words fell unheeded into the empty air.

Chapter Three

Jake Rossiter parked his car at an angle on the Fergusons' gravel drive, flung the door open and slid out easily. It was now three days since the theft of the Coalport vase, and it seemed the police were still none the wiser as to who the culprit was.

Jake's eyes darkened, his thoughts troubled. The police may be none the wiser, but Lauren James had her suspicions, all right. Or was that all just a smokescreen, to distract attention away from herself? He slammed the car door shut with considerable force. Pity, she'd seemed so down to earth, seemed to have her head screwed on the right way. Not to mention the fact that he'd really enjoyed her company the other night.

Shame that young Lauren had to go shooting her mouth off every now and then — no wonder he'd been so sorely tempted to silence her with a kiss the other night, although, with hindsight, he knew he'd been right not to. That would have been deliberately courting danger, and besides, she seemed infatuated with that slimy Stephen Hughes. Still, she was a strikingly attractive young woman. Even now, an image came to him of large, leaf-green eyes gazing impudently at him from beneath dancing, golden-brown curls. Jake shook his head roughly, so the image dissolved and vanished.

He glanced briskly at his watch — ten past two. Now he was late, yet again. He had a responsibility, a job to carry out that he had no intention of shirking. Jake set off at a brisk jog towards the large house, his feet crunching on the gravel.

Meanwhile, Lauren glanced at the kitchen clock, then set her tea-cup down in its saucer.

"Well, thanks for the tea, Maggie."

"Not at all," Maggie demurred. "I enjoyed our chat."

"Me, too," Lauren agreed.

It was true. She had chatted to her friend, Sally, on the phone last night but it wasn't the same as a face-to-face encounter. Maggie Foster had a comforting air of normality about her which helped

Lauren forget about the unpleasantness of the burglaries, being questioned by the police and having her room searched, fruitlessly, of course. The police had once again found no fingerprints at the scene of the crime, either.

"I could sit here all day," Lauren admitted, "but I suppose I'd better go and see if that young scamp's returned from the land of nod. He'll never go off to sleep tonight if he has too long now."

"Good luck," Maggie called with a smile.

"Thanks," Lauren called back, already halfway up the sweeping main staircase.

"Daniel," she said softly, entering the little boy's bedroom through its half-opened door a couple of minutes later.

In the dimness all was quiet and still. Lauren drew the curtains, releasing a shaft of light to fall across the room. Then she turned towards the bed. As she did so, her heart plummeted. The bed was empty! Quickly, she spun round, scanning the room. It, too, was empty.

"Daniel!" Lauren called again, her heart beginning to pound, her habitual calm beginning to disperse. "Daniel, sweetheart, where are you?"

As Lauren raced back down the staircase, her mind was racing, too. Oh, why had she stayed an extra two minutes chatting with Maggie? Why hadn't she gone straight up to check on Daniel on the dot of quarter past two, as she should have done? Instead, Daniel had woken up by himself, and gone off somewhere, alone.

As Lauren reached the ground floor and paused, the silence of the big, old house echoed around her. Of course, it was Christine's afternoon at the Women's Institute, Janey was at college and Geoffrey was out seeing a client. They had entrusted their little boy's care to her, and this was how she repaid them! She'd always been one hundred per cent reliable in the past.

Frantic, Lauren dashed down the gloomy corridors, pausing to stick her head through any open doorways. She checked the sitting-room, the downstairs toilet, Geoffrey's study, until finally, she was back in the kitchen, where Maggie was washing up. Lauren burst into the room.

"Oh, Maggie, something dreadful's happened!"

"Oh, my dear, what is it?"

Maggie's pale hazel eyes were full of concern.

"It's Daniel. I can't find him anywhere!"

"He wasn't in his bedroom when you went up?"

"No. Oh, Maggie, I must find him."

Lauren rushed back out of the kitchen.

"Hang on a minute — Lauren?" Maggie called as she was leaving, but Lauren was already heading for the front door.

Lauren couldn't believe it when she set foot outside the Fergusons' huge oak front door, and saw Jake Rossiter, casually dressed in jeans and a grey cotton shirt, calmly strapping Daniel into a seat in the back of his open-topped car. She ran helter-skelter down the steps to the gravel drive.

"What on earth do you think you're doing?" she exploded, as she reached the car.

Startled, Jake turned round. He quickly recovered his composure.

"What does it look like I'm doing?"

"Kidnapping Daniel?" Lauren suggested pointedly, between rapid breaths, rushing over to comfort the little boy.

Jake actually laughed at this, throwing back his head, his dark eyes twinkling with amusement.

"Oh, Lauren, you really must do something about that over-active imagination of yours!"

"Well?" Lauren demanded, relief and confusion making her belligerent. "Have you got a better explanation?"

"Well, yes."

"I went to Daniel's room to wake him up from his afternoon sleep, and he wasn't there. Then I find you about to whisk him off in your car, without so much as a by-your-leave!"

Jake turned away from the car, his smile fading as realisation dawned.

"Oh, Lauren, did no-one tell you?"

"Tell me what?" Lauren snapped.

"It's a standing arrangement with the Fergusons. I have Daniel every Thursday afternoon. He is my godson, after all."

Lauren's eyes lightened in understanding.

"Your godson?"

But she still felt in no mood to forgive and forget.

"So you just thought you'd go in and take him from his bed without checking with me first?"

"I'm sorry, Lauren. I went up to Daniel's room, like I always do, and he was awake and up, waiting for me. I tried to find you to tell you we were off, but when I couldn't, I assumed you knew anyway and decided we might as well just go. I suppose, with hindsight, it was rather thought-less of me."

"Rather thoughtless," Lauren echoed, thinking that this was the understatement of the century as tears welled ominously in her blue eyes. "I was beside myself with worry."

The front door of the house opened and Maggie Foster appeared.

"Oh, there you are, Lauren! I was trying to find you to tell you that I remembered it was Jake's day for having Daniel, but it looks like you already know."

"Yes, thank you, Maggie."

Lauren managed a wobbly smile as Maggie disappeared back indoors.

"Are you all right, Daniel?" she asked her young charge.

"Yes, all right."

The little boy smiled, looking delighted to be ensconced in the animal-patterned seat in Jake's sports car, clutching his plastic toy tiger. He held out his arms for a hug and Lauren obliged.

"See?" Jake asked. "Daniel's fine. There's no harm done."

"I know. I was just so worried."

Suddenly Jake's deep voice was all con-cern.

"There's no need to cry."

He moved towards her, putting a huge, bear-like arm around her shoulders. But his concern was the last thing Lauren needed. At the sound of a kind voice, her brave façade gave way, and she dissolved into tears. Jake said nothing, just gently turned her, so that she was able to cry into his shoulder.

"What's a matter?" Lauren heard Daniel's voice asking.

"It's all right, Dan," Jake replied over her head. "Lauren's just a bit upset. She'll be fine in a minute."

The sound of Daniel's voice reminded Lauren abruptly of her responsibilities, and she made an effort to pull herself together. She extracted her head from the soft cotton of Jake's shirt.

"See, Daniel? I'm fine now," she said and smiled.

Jake looked at her with concern for a moment, an expression in his dark brown eyes that made Lauren's heart skip a beat. Then he bent towards her again, and gently smoothed away a teardrop from each cheek.

"I really am sorry for behaving like a thoughtless pig," he said, his usual self-assured manner completely dispersed. "Will you ever forgive me?"

59

Lauren was about to tell him that she did forgive him, then and there, but as she opened her mouth, the words died in her throat. Of course, she had forgotten that Jake Rossiter was a professionally-charming man. Right at this moment he was probably putting on an act, an act of concern, when all he was really concerned about was protecting his own interests. Suddenly Lauren recalled her suspicions about him, and gave an involuntary shiver.

"Forgive you?" she asked, her voice low. "I wouldn't hold your breath." She turned to the little boy, forcing a brighter tone. "Be a good boy for Uncle Jake, Daniel, and I'll see you later."

Lauren then turned and walked briskly back up the steps, before she was forced to meet Jake Rossiter's dark, questioning gaze.

That night was her night off, and Lauren had arranged to meet Sally for a drink in Gorse Hill. At the weekend, she would have the whole Sunday to herself, and planned to go home and spend some time with her parents.

The warm spell was continuing and it was another balmy, summer evening. Lauren dressed in a long, cool cream cotton skirt and light blue fitted top and set off on the short walk down winding, undulating roads to the pub where she and Sally had agreed to meet, situated just outside the village, towards the coast. As she walked, Lauren's thoughts drifted back to the complicated, enigmatic Jake Rossiter and her suspicions about him.

When Lauren arrived at the Kingston Arms she saw Sally's familiar yellow car already in the large carpark and her heavy heart lifted at the sight of it. As soon as she entered the dim, olde-worlde pub, with its low ceilings and thick, wooden beams, Lauren saw Sally herself, sitting on a bar stool nursing her habitual soft drink. Her petite figure was clad in a shocking pink top and denim shorts, the top clashing wildly with Sally's shoulder-length red hair, yet somehow managing to make her look, as usual, strikingly attractive. As if by instinct, Sally spun round.

"And what time do you call this, Miss James?" she asked with mock sternness, tapping her watch.

In surprise, Lauren glanced at her watch. She was, indeed, a couple of minutes late, a rare occurrence for her, normally such a punctual person.

"Sorry, Sal," she threw back. "I guess I must have been so deep in my thoughts I walked too slowly. Anyway, it's good to see you."

Sally slipped off the stool and she and Lauren hugged each other fondly.

"You, too," Sally agreed. "It seems like months since I've seen you and it isn't even a week." When she had ordered Lauren a tomato juice, she said, "Let's go and sit in the garden. It's stifling in here tonight."

The garden of the Kingston Arms was breathtaking, stretching almost to where the land descended to the hazy sea. They found an empty wooden table and sat down.

"So, tell me, Sal, how's things with you?" Lauren asked.

"Well, to begin with, things have been rather interesting at work lately."

Sally proceeded to tell her, at great length, about the in-fighting at the bank where she worked, her car's recent MOT, and a dishy new Italian temp at work called Dino, whom Sally had set her sights on.

"Anyway," Sally said eventually, pausing for a sip of her drink, "I won't let you distract me with any more questions about myself. What about you? How's the new job, and what are these thoughts you were so deep in that they made you late?"

Lauren's mouth twisted wryly.

"There's so much to tell, I don't know where to start."

"I'll help you then. I'll ask you a question, and you give me a one-word answer."

Lauren sighed, but she was used to Sally's love of game-playing.

"OK."

"House?" Sally questioned.

Lauren considered.

"Old. A bit creepy."

"I said one word," Sally warned. "People?"

"Daniel's a darling, and the rest of them are very nice, even the family vet," Lauren replied promptly, adding, "The neighbour's the only fly in the ointment."

"Neighbour?"

Now, how to sum up Jake Rossiter in one word? Numerous options drifted through Lauren's mind — arrogant, good-looking, argumentative, attractive. He had been kind the other day, too, but then that had probably been an act.

"Untrustworthy."

But Lauren had no desire to dwell on the subject of Jake.

"But thankfully the rest of them are OK," she babbled on. "A bit on their guard sometimes, but that's probably because of what's going on up there."

"You're not very good at this game, are you?" Sally reproved. "So tell me what's going on there. It sounds most intriguing."

Lauren stirred her tomato juice dreamily with the swizzle stick.

"I don't know if I should tell you. I vowed I wouldn't tell my mum."

Sally frowned at this.

"Come on, Lauren," she urged, her voice gentler now. "If there's something wrong I think you should tell me. After all, a problem shared is a problem halved."

"Well, there have been these burglaries up at the house."

Sally's hazel eyes widened.

"Burglaries? How many?"

"Two. Some valuable antiques have been stolen. I've got a horrible feeling the Fergusons suspect me. I feel like I'm being watched twenty-four hours a day, and any day now I could be out of a job."

"Oh, Laurie, that's awful," Sally breathed, laying a hand over her friend's on the table. "So they've got no idea who did it?"

"No." Lauren hesitated. "But I've got my suspicions."

"Who?"

Lauren grimaced.

"This brings us back to the neighbour again."

"Male?" Sally fired at her.

"Yes. He's an antiques dealer, you see, and Mr Ferguson's best friend!"

"Attractive?"

"Yes, I suppose so. Honestly, Sally," Lauren blustered, "you've got a one-track mind."

"Thought so," Sally said with satisfaction. "It's always the attractive ones you can't trust. Shame, though, because maybe if things had been different you and he might have . . ."

She left her sentence unfinished, leaving Lauren to draw her own conclusions. Lauren flushed.

"I don't think so, Sally."

"As it is, though," Sally surged on, "you'll just have to prove the man's guilt. It's the only way you'll save your own skin," she added, seeing the look in Lauren's eyes. "I'll get some more drinks," she went on, "and we'll draw up a plan of action. It's obvious the police won't have searched him, what with him being Mr Ferguson's best friend. You'll have to get into his house somehow."

Lauren gasped.

"No, Sally!"

But Sally went on, "And locate the stolen goods, don't you see?"

Watching her friend's retreating back, Lauren sighed again. Of course, she would like to be able to prove her innocence, but she didn't want to be involved with anything as underhand as Sally had suggested. She was reluctant to get involved with any crazy scheme that would jeopardise her job, put her in danger, or entangle her more closely with the devious, scheming yet oh-so-attractive Jake Rossiter.

That night, as she tossed and turned in her bed, Lauren's thoughts were dominated by Sally's plan. No, it was fundamentally wrong to break into someone's house. She couldn't do it, she decided.

She was still brooding the following morning in the sun-dappled kitchen, when Jake Rossiter breezed in, demanding to know where Geoffrey could be found. Indignantly, Lauren put down the spoonful of cereal she was about to feed Daniel.

"How did you get in? It's Maggie's day off, and I'm sure I didn't hear the doorbell ring."

Jake smiled disarmingly, a smile that lit up the depths of his dark eyes.

"I know Maggie and Derek are off on Fridays, so I took the liberty of letting myself in the back way. I hope you don't mind."

Lauren was infuriated, but she just said evenly, "It doesn't seem as if I have any choice in the matter, anyway," and went back to feeding Daniel.

Thankfully at that moment Geoffrey came in.

"Out of the way, folks," he said cheerfully. "I need my morning caffeine fix and there's no Maggie this morning. I don't know, these impudent staff with their requests for time off!" he joked.

"I know," Jake added, with a wink at Lauren. "How they have the audacity to think they've got the right to a life of their own."

Lauren felt unnerved by the look of conspiratorial humour in his eyes, so she looked away.

"More," Daniel demanded, fortunately giving her the excuse to concentrate on getting the little boy's breakfast inside him.

"So, Geoff," Jake was saying, going over to Geoffrey as he spooned ground coffee into the percolator, "how about a game of squash on Sunday afternoon?"

"OK, great," Geoffrey replied, "though I expect you'll thrash me as usual!"

"Oh, I wouldn't bet on it," Jake replied

airily. "I'll book a court for, say, four-thirty then."

"Fine. Should be back in time for the Antiques Roadshow."

Then Geoffrey glanced over at Lauren.

"Maybe I should enlist you to join my side on the squash court, Lauren." He smiled. "I could do with all the help I can get against our Mr Rossiter."

"I think," Lauren said and smiled back, "that Daniel here would be more use to you. Badminton's more my game, I'm afraid."

"Surely not," Jake protested, joining in the banter. "I'm sure you're a demon with a squash racquet, Lauren. And besides, I'm sure you'd enjoy annihilating me as much on court as you do off."

Lauren met his eyes for a moment, unsure whether he was joking or serious. She began to feel uncomfortable.

"More!" Daniel demanded.

"Sorry, sweetheart," Lauren muttered in relief, busying herself.

It was only after Jake had rushed off to open his shop, and Geoffrey, too, had taken his coffee and retreated, that something clicked and Lauren's mind started to work overtime. Sunday was her day off, and she was going to her parents' for lunch. As long as she left their house by four-thirty, she should have plenty of time to get back to Gorse Hill and search Jake's house for the stolen antiques.

The next moment, Lauren was shocked at herself. How could she have contemplated such a deceitful, underhand thing? No, she couldn't do it. Uneasily, Lauren put down her own slice of toast untouched, her normally healthy appetite completely gone.

When Sunday came, Lauren's feelings were dominated by excitement about seeing her family again. At the James' family home she was joyfully reunited with her mother, father and twin younger brothers, Michael and Christopher.

Lauren enjoyed one of her mother's excellent roast dinners and afterwards sat around with the family chatting about her new job and the family news, and reading the Sunday papers. She was shocked when she happened to glance at her watch and noticed that it was nearly four o'clock.

"Goodness, is that the time?" she exclaimed. "Sorry, Mum, Dad, but I suppose I ought to be getting back."

She wanted to be back in time to tidy her room, wash some of her clothes and hang them out to dry, and generally settle back into the Ferguson house before night-fall.

Carole James glanced up from her magazine, eyes concerned.

"Already, love? I hope those Fergusons aren't slave-drivers."

"No, of course not."

Then Lauren's eyes narrowed in suspicion.

"What's up? This isn't anything to do with what happened to my great-grandmother is it, Mum?"

"Let's not discuss poor Violet just now, darling," Carole James said quickly, leaving Lauren more curious than ever as to what had happened to her ancestor. "I'm just worried the Fergusons are working you too hard, that's all."

"Well, they're not," Lauren soothed her mother. "I want to get back for my own reasons. There are a couple of things I want to sort out."

Paul James, a tall, thin man with cropped hair the same distinctive colour as his daughter's, got to his feet.

"In that case I'll give you a lift then, Laurie," he said evenly.

"Don't worry, Dad, I'll be fine," Lauren started to protest.

"It'll be no problem, love," he insisted

calmly. "The sky looks ominous. This weather could break at any moment. Come on."

A few minutes later, Lauren had said her fond goodbyes to her father and stuck her head through the Ferguson's sitting-room door to let them know she was back.

"Hello, Lauren," Christine greeted her.

Daniel scrambled down from the settee beside his mother, coming to fling his arms around Lauren's legs.

"Hi, Daniel," Lauren said fondly, hugging him back. "Hello, Christine," she added with a grin. "It's quiet in here," she observed.

"Yes, Janey's over at the stables and Geoffrey's out playing squash with Jake," Christine said.

"Funny how the men make most of the noise, isn't it?" Lauren joked.

Inwardly she recalled with a pang that Jake's house was currently unoccupied and thus free for searching. Cursing Sally, she dismissed the traitorous thought.

"Want tiger!" Daniel demanded, breaking into her thoughts.

"He's been saying that all afternoon, and I'm blessed if I know what he's talking about," Christine said with a sigh.

An image came into Lauren's mind of

Daniel sitting in the back of Jake's car, clutching his large plastic toy tiger.

"He seems very fond of his toy tiger lately. I last saw him with it when Jake was taking him out the other afternoon."

"Then I bet he's left it at Jake's house," Christine said.

"Want tiger!" Daniel repeated. "Want tiger!"

"Lauren," Christine said slowly, "I don't suppose you'd be a dear and pop over to Jake's house and see if you can find the blasted thing?"

Instantly Lauren's face coloured.

"But Jake's out at the moment, playing squash with Geoffrey."

"I know, but you could let yourself in. He keeps a spare front door key buried in the big stone urn to the left of the door."

With the burglaries and all the attendant mistrust in mind, Lauren felt uncomfortable.

"Oh, no, I couldn't, Mrs Ferguson, not without Mr Rossiter's permission."

Christine's tanned, handsome face broke into a beaming smile.

"Nonsense! Of course Jake won't mind. We're in and out of each other's houses all the time."

"Want tiger!" Daniel demanded again.

"Oh, OK then," Lauren said reluctantly. She tried to push Sally's plan from her mind.

"Thanks, Lauren," Christine said in relief. "You're a lifesaver."

Lauren quickly left the house, wanting to get this over with as soon as possible. There was an unfamiliar car in the Fergusons' drive as she left, but only her subconscious registered it, preoccupied as she was.

A plaque beside the large, white-painted front door proclaimed Jake's residence to be called Davenham House. It was a big, sprawling house, built of the local grey stone, with matching grey roof slates, speckled with age and lichen. Pointed gables rose up on each side of the house, each topped with an ornate, Victorian stone globe, and there was a cluster of chimneys of various sizes in the centre of the roof. It was an unusual, romantic-looking house, Lauren thought to herself.

After scrabbling about in potting compost for a couple of minutes, Lauren located the key. Wiping a few traces of earth from it, she inserted it into the front door and swung it open, her heart pounding. Once she was inside the comparative gloom of the front hall, its tiled floor dappled with red and green light from the coloured glass in the door, she glanced at her watch. Good, only just gone half past four. She should have time to find the wretched tiger and get out of there quick, before Jake returned. But where to start?

Feeling intensely uneasy, Lauren located Jake's plush, comfortable sitting-room and began to search. Overhead she heard a rumble of thunder. So her father had been right, she thought, busying herself. But, after a few minutes, she hadn't found the toy anywhere, and moved on to the surprisingly white, minimalist kitchen. She heard another rumble and saw, through the window, lightning slash the glowering sky, illuminating the darkened room. Now, where was the most likely place Daniel would have left his toy? The thought turned traitorous. Where was the most likely place Jake would have hidden stolen antiques?

Creeping along the passageway, she passed what looked like his study and heard the rain battering its window. Peering inside, Lauren was drawn by strange magnetism towards the large, antique mahogany desk. A Coalport vase wouldn't fit in one of its drawers, but a silver card-case was a different matter.

Lauren scowled. She wasn't looking for a card-case, she was looking for Daniel's toy tiger! Heart pounding, she tried one of the drawers, half-expecting it to be locked. It slid open, revealing nothing more sinister than envelopes and postage stamps.

Lauren slammed the drawer shut, filled with shame and remorse. She'd never done anything underhand in her life before, never stolen so much as a penny chew from the corner shop. Besides, a more down-to-earth voice in her head added, it was a fool's errand anyway. If Jake Rossiter had stolen the Fergusons' antiques, he was far more likely to have locked them in a safe somewhere, or even in his Ecclesdon shop. And she still hadn't found Daniel's toy tiger. So what did she do now? Panicking, Lauren reached for the phone on Jake's desk and dialled the Fergusons' number. Christine answered on the second ring.

"Oh, Christine," Lauren gabbled, "I'm ringing from Jake's house. I'll pay him for the call, of course. The thing is, I still can't find Daniel's tiger!"

"Oh, Lauren," Christine said. "I was about to ring Jake's house myself, and tell you. Daniel's found his tiger. It was in his toy-box all along!"

75

"Oh, thank goodness," Lauren said.

Now maybe she could get out of here. It was as Lauren set the phone down that she heard the distant but unmistakable rasp of a key in the front door. Stupidly, she glanced at her watch. Only quarter to five! Jake shouldn't be back yet! In that moment she thought about hiding, but sensed it was futile. Somehow her legs managed to carry her out of Jake's study and back to the hall to face the music.

"Hello, Jake."

She'd been expecting him of course, but still at the sight of him her heart lurched. He looked flushed and handsome in shorts and a sports top, dark curls tousled, a barrel bag slung over one shoulder. His brows drew together as he registered her intruding presence.

"Lauren!" he exclaimed, before she could offer an explanation. "What on earth are you doing here?"

Chapter Four

Eventually Lauren found her tongue, and
stammered, "It — it's not what it looks like.
Christine said you wouldn't mind if I let myself in. She told me where you keep your
front door key. I'm terribly sorry," Lauren
added awkwardly.

Jake dropped his sports bag to the
ground with a thud.

"Christine's right. I don't mind anyone
from the Ferguson household letting themselves in. They're not only excellent neighbours, they're close friends, too. Yes, feel
free to let yourself in, Lauren, make yourself at home. Oh," he added, his tone de-
ceptively light, "I see you already have."

"I'm sorry," Lauren said again, feeling
her face flush with embarrassment.

"I said it's fine, Lauren. I really don't
mind. I just wondered," he went on, eyeing
her, "why it was you came."

"I didn't think you'd be in. I thought you were playing squash at four-thirty."

Momentarily Jake frowned, then it cleared.

"I did originally intend to book the court for then, but they didn't have any so I had to settle for three-thirty instead."

He gazed expectantly at Lauren, awaiting her explanation.

"I came to get Daniel's toy tiger. He left it here the other day."

Jake glanced pointedly at Lauren's empty hands.

"So?" he prompted, his tone almost insolent. "Where is it?"

"I thought it was here, but I was mistaken."

Lauren waited for Jake's verbal onslaught, but he just said, in a low voice, "Are you sure this flimsy story about Daniel's toy isn't just a pretext for your coming here for some other reason?"

Lauren's heart lurched. So Jake had jumped to conclusions, assuming she had come here to snoop around his house, an assumption that was uncomfortably close to the truth.

"Well?" Jake demanded impatiently.

"I suppose, in a way, you're right," Lauren replied slowly.

"I am?" Jake asked sharply. "What do you mean exactly, Lauren? What's the real reason you came here?"

Lauren knew she was trapped, cornered. An idea occurred to her.

Without thinking she answered quickly, "The real reason I came here was, if I'm honest, to see you. I thought I'd wait till you got back."

Now why had she said that, Lauren wondered, indignant at herself. To her surprise, Jake smiled, a smile that lit up his glinting, treacle-dark eyes.

"Really?" he asked, seeming genuinely pleased. "You came to see me? Well, that's fantastic."

His habitual self-assurance returned.

"But you don't have to be shy about it, Lauren. If you wanted to come and see me, you could have just come straight out and said so."

Ashamed of herself, Lauren found herself peeping coquettishly up at him, through her dark lashes.

"Well, I know things haven't always been easy between us, and I just felt I wanted to come and offer an olive branch."

Lauren couldn't believe the untruths that were spouting from her lips. She was normally wary of the tiniest white lie. Jake was still smiling broadly.

"Well, I must say I'm delighted to hear it. I'm just surprised. I thought you were enamoured with that Hughes chap."

"Stephen?" Lauren asked unsteadily.

To her surprise, she realised it was the first time in several days she had thought of Stephen Hughes.

"Oh, no," she said quickly. "Stephen and I are just friends."

Jake was still grinning at her.

"I've always enjoyed your company, Lauren, and I've made no secret of the fact. But perhaps you'd just excuse me while I go and grab a quick shower. I'm not exactly in a fit state for visitors at the moment."

"Oh, well, I must be going anyway. I only popped round quickly. Christine will be wondering where I am."

Jake frowned.

"Sunday's your day off, isn't it?"

"How did you know that?" Lauren asked, taken aback.

Grinning, Jake tapped his nose and said, "Oh, I know these things."

Lauren shivered involuntarily, reminded that Jake Rossiter was a mysterious, enigmatic man. There was a lot she didn't know about him.

"As I said," Lauren gabbled nervously,

"I really must be going."

Momentarily they both fell silent, gazing at each other. Jake was looking at her in a different way, as if what she'd said about her reasons for coming here had altered the relationship between them. Then he took a step towards her. He raised his right hand, cupping her cheek, and drew her towards him. Then he kissed her, full on the mouth. Intoxicated by his closeness, Lauren found herself kissing him back, and suddenly she realised that her attraction to Stephen Hughes was as nothing compared to what she felt towards Jake. When they drew apart, she gazed at him, stunned. Unable to believe what had happened, Lauren raised her hand to her lips, touching them as they still tingled with awareness.

"I'm sorry," Jake said eventually. "That shouldn't have happened."

Lauren's heart plummeted with disappointment, but good sense told her that he was right — they should never have kissed. It was madness.

"No," she agreed weakly.

The expression in Jake's eyes softened.

"I don't mean I don't like you, or find you unattractive, Lauren, far from it. I just think we should take things more slowly."

"Absolutely."

Suddenly Lauren had come to her senses, realising the last thing she wanted was to start a relationship with Jake Rossiter, however pleasant his kisses were.

"In fact," she ventured mischievously, "perhaps we should take things so slowly that they don't proceed at all."

"I've got an idea," Jake said, ignoring her. "I'm going to another antiques fair next Sunday, in Wareham."

"Oh, that'll be nice for you," Lauren replied, her confidence returning.

Jake surged on, as if she hadn't spoken.

"Why don't you come with me? It'll give us a chance to get to know each other better."

Part of Lauren felt that this was the last thing she wanted, but aware of the pretext she had given Jake for visiting his house that day, was aware that she could hardly tell him this.

"I don't know," she prevaricated.

"Go on," Jake coaxed. "You said you wanted us to be friends."

What would Sally do in this situation, Lauren asked herself desperately, knowing exactly what Sally would do. She would go to the fair, and use it as an opportunity to find out more about Jake Rossiter and his business dealings, above and below board.

"OK," Lauren said slowly. "OK, you're on."

Fortunately, the rain eased off soon after that, and Lauren was able to make a quick dash back to Misty Towers. The unfamiliar car that she'd noted before was still in the drive. As she mounted the wet steps the front door opened and to her surprise, Stephen Hughes came out. He looked momentarily nonplussed to see her, then his face broke into a wide smile.

"Lauren!" he exclaimed. "How lovely to see you!"

"I didn't expect to see you here on a Sunday," she said, curiously.

Stephen's smile faded a little.

"Yes, well, Christine phoned to say one of the horses was a bit off-colour, and I didn't have anything else on, so I came round."

"Oh, well, it was nice talking to you," Lauren said, poised to go indoors.

"You, too," Stephen replied, jogging down the remaining steps. "And I haven't forgotten about taking you out on the boat," he called.

"I'll be looking forward to it," Lauren called back, though, inwardly, she couldn't help wondering why this was somehow not strictly true.

That day's thunderstorm seemed to clear the air, and the brilliant sunshine resumed for the whole of the week that followed, although the air was a little fresher than before. Sally phoned her on the Monday evening, eager to know if Lauren had managed to search the house of the dishy neighbour yet. Lauren had taken the call in the now-empty kitchen and, hearing Sally's voice, she leaned against the kitchen door, easing it shut with her shoulder.

"Oh, Sally," she hissed, her voice little more than a whisper, "you know I never intended to get involved with your wretched scheme, but I happened to be round at Jake's house yesterday."

"Why?" Sally asked suspiciously.

"To cut a long story short, I was looking for Daniel's toy tiger. Only, while I was there, I kept thinking about your mad plan."

"So, you had a quick look. Did you find anything?" Sally demanded.

"No," Lauren whispered, "and the worst of it, Jake arrived back and found me in his house."

"Really?" Sally breathed. "What did he do?"

Lauren took an unsteady breath, recalling the kiss. She didn't want to mention that now.

"The long and the short of it is," she said hastily, "I ended up agreeing to go to an antiques fair with him next week."

"And you still don't know if he's innocent or guilty?"

"No," Lauren admitted.

"Oh, I'd be careful if I was you, Laurie," Sally said, to Lauren's surprise. "Supposing this Jake bloke is guilty. He probably plans to win you over with a charm offensive. Take my advice. The only way you'll be safe is if you make it quite clear you're going out together purely as friends."

"OK. Hang on."

Lauren could hear footsteps coming down the passageway.

"I'll have to go, Sal, someone's coming."

"Take care, Laurie! And don't do anything I wouldn't do."

On the day of the antiques fair, Lauren rose early. Mindful of Sally's advice, not wanting to give Jake the wrong idea, she dressed in her comfortable old denim skirt and a light blue top. After all, she was loathe for him to think she had made any effort on his behalf! Jake had arranged to pick her up at half past seven in the morning.

85

For once Jake was on time, pulling up on the Fergusons' gravel drive on the dot of seven thirty.

"Here, allow me," Jake said, leaping out of his side of the open tourer to open the passenger door for her.

In spite of herself, Lauren noted that he was smarter than her but not too smart, in loose, stone-coloured trousers, and a casual dark blue shirt.

"No, it's fine, honestly," Lauren protested, embarrassed. "I'm perfectly capable of opening a car door for myself, Jake."

"And to think it's usually you women who complain that the age of chivalry is dead," Jake commented light-heartedly as he helped her into her seat. "You look lovely, by the way, Lauren," he added, making her feel more uncomfortable than ever.

"Not as smart as you," she replied, adding, "I didn't realise you had to dress up for these fairs."

"I always feel it's best to make a good impression, good for business, you understand," Jake replied, sliding back into his seat and slamming the car door. "But I meant what I said. You do look lovely. Just right."

Suddenly Lauren had had enough, and wanted to set the record straight.

"It's OK, Jake," she said, turning to him as he slid his key into the ignition, "you don't have to lay it on so thick." She laughed nervously. "It's not as if we're on a date or anything."

"Oh, no, of course not," Jake answered back. "Nothing as heavy as that. But we're two people who like each other, right?"

Lauren hesitated.

"Well . . ."

Jake's mouth twisted with ill-concealed impatience.

"Come on, Lauren, you came round to my house last week expressly to tell me as much."

Whoops, so she had. Remembering her white lie, Lauren conceded.

"OK, yes, I like you," and as she said it, she realised that maybe it was true. Jake's grin was full of warmth this time.

"Great, we like each other. Now let's just have a nice time today, see how things go, and not rush into anything, OK?"

"OK," Lauren agreed cautiously.

It was a beautiful morning, and the Dorset countryside looked stunning in the clear sunlight as they took the main road through undulating hills, with the occasional vista of sparkling sea appearing on the horizon.

"Let's talk about something else," Lauren said as they drove along.

"OK, fine," Jake said. "Let's get back to basics, shall we? Tell me about your family. Have they lived round here long?"

"Oh, yes," she replied. "The James' family is good old Dorset stock. My mum and dad both come from Ecclesdon."

"Any brothers or sisters?"

Lauren wrinkled her nose.

"Younger twin brothers, Mike and Chris. They're nineteen now, but I still think of them as toddlers in nappies. The terrible twins, I used to call them. I love them both dearly, of course," she added. "How about your family?"

"I'm originally from Dorchester," he replied. "My parents still live there. My father's in the antiques trade, too. He's done rather well for himself. I moved down here, let's see, eleven years ago now. And, before you ask, I've got one younger brother, Peter. He lives in Australia," he concluded.

"And what does Peter do for a living?" Lauren asked.

"Do?" Jake queried rhetorically. "Lie on the beach? Work on his tan? Without being rude, you could say that Pete is the original beach bum."

As they passed through the picturesque

village of Corfe Castle, Lauren thought that she would be very intrigued to meet this Peter. The old ruined castle rose dramatically from the early-morning haze as they rounded the bend, then finally they crossed the River Frome to arrive in the old market town of Wareham.

"See?" Jake said later in a low voice close to her ear, as they wandered around the stalls in the old market place. "Not a speck of dust in sight."

"No, Jake," Lauren replied evenly.

She was beginning to heartily regret an ill-chosen remark about dusty, old antiques. She paused at a stall adorned with an array of gleaming chinaware as a piece caught her eye.

"Hey, that's pretty," she said, pointing.

"Pretty!" Jake echoed, amused. "Here, let me have a look."

Jake leaned closer to the stall to examine the piece Lauren had indicated. It was what looked like a small china watering can, with a gold-painted spout and handle, its body decorated with a delicately-painted bouquet of flowers.

"There's no need to mock," Lauren said indignantly. "I'd be the first to admit I'm no expert. I was just saying that I liked it."

Jake's expression was now serious as he inspected the piece.

"May I, Bob?" he asked the jovial-looking, middle-aged stallholder.

"Go ahead, Jake," the man replied with a wink at Lauren.

After turning it carefully over in his hands for a minute or so, Jake said, "What do you want for it, Bob?"

"Two fifty," the stallholder replied, like a shot.

Lauren gasped. Even she knew that he meant two hundred and fifty pounds, rather than two pounds fifty pence.

"Come on now, Bob," Jake was saying with a disarming grin. "What's your best price?"

"All right then, two-two five, as it's you, Jake."

"I was thinking more like one eighty," Jake haggled.

Bob shook his head.

"Two ten."

"How about a nice round two?" Jake suggested.

Bob hesitated for what seemed like an eternity.

Finally he said, "Go on then. Two hundred."

"Done," Jake said, shaking the man's

hand before rummaging in his pocket for his wallet and producing a wad of slightly-crumpled notes.

"You'll do me out of house and home, Jake Rossiter."

Lauren watched the whole exchange open-jawed. Sure, she mused, Jake had beaten the man's price right down, but that hardly made him a criminal, did it? As they left the stall, Jake carrying his purchase, wrapped in tissue paper and nestling in a cardboard box, Lauren turned to him, wide-eyed.

"Two hundred pounds? You spend two hundred pounds, at the drop of a hat? That's almost a week's wages, to me."

Jake leaned close to her, his voice a whisper.

"Thanks to you, Lauren, I'm now the proud owner of a Minton cabinet watering can. This is a very rare piece, could fetch anything from three to five hundred pounds at auction. I know you're new to this game, but you certainly have an eye for a bargain."

"But all I said was that I liked it," Lauren murmured, bemused.

"And in doing so earned me a couple of hundred pounds. Not bad for a few min-utes' work. In fact, I could kiss you. No, I will kiss you."

And with that, he leaned forward, amidst the bustle of the crowded market-place, and kissed Lauren firmly on the lips. Stunned, Lauren was powerless to resist.

"Two hundred pounds," she breathed dazedly, thinking excitedly of Jake's potential profit on the purchase. "Yes, I like this," she announced in some surprise. "I think I could get used to it."

"What, the kiss?" Jake asked roguishly. "Or the thrill of the antiques' trade?"

"You know exactly what I meant," Lauren reproved him firmly, but she was unable to suppress the twinkle in her green eyes.

"What a team!" Jake was going on, cradling the precious cardboard box. "Maybe we should go into partnership," he teased. "You bargain-spotting, me haggling."

To her surprise, she was having such a good time that she didn't want the day to end. At that moment she didn't really care whether Jake Rossiter was of dubious character or not. She had always had appalling taste in men, she thought wryly. And, deep down, she found herself hoping fervently that no more antiques would go missing from Misty Towers.

Lauren enjoyed herself so much that the rest of the day passed in a flash.

It seemed as though the feeling was mutual, because as Jake dropped her back at the Fergusons' that evening, he turned to her in the car and said, "Thank you for a wonderful day, Lauren."

"Thank you, too. It's been nice," Lauren replied, more cautiously.

Jake turned to rummage behind his carseat, retrieving a tissue-paper wrapped package. He handed it to Lauren.

"I'd like you to take this."

As soon as Lauren peeled back the edge of the tissue paper she knew what it was.

"The Minton watering-can?" she gasped. "No, Jake, I couldn't possibly."

"But you deserve it," Jake argued back. "You spotted it, after all."

But Lauren stood firm.

"No, thank you, Jake," she said quietly. "It's extremely generous of you, but I couldn't take it."

It wasn't just the money. She had no desire to be bought over by any of Jake's pretty trinkets. She wasn't even sure what he was trying to buy — her agreement to going on a second date, or maybe even her silence regarding the robberies?

"Very well, Lauren," Jake had said, defeated, and mildly disappointed, "have it your way. But I still had a wonderful day."

"Me, too," Lauren admitted, and she meant it.

The following Friday, a listless-looking, scruffily-dressed Janey drifted into the kitchen as Lauren was clearing away Daniel's breakfast.

"What's up?" Lauren asked. "No college this morning?"

"I've got a free period Friday mornings. I'm going in later. It's the last day before the holidays," Janey replied, fetching a can of juice from the fridge. "No, I've just been over to the stables. Poor old Saladin wouldn't touch his breakfast this morning, so I gave him a carrot instead. It's not like Saladin to refuse his breakfast. I'm a bit worried about him."

"Well, why don't you call Stephen?" Lauren asked.

Janey's face lengthened.

"I can't. Stephen's away at the moment, some veterinary seminar up in Newcastle. He's not back till Monday."

"Maybe that's Saladin's problem," Janey mused. "He's missing Stephen."

"Who's missing Stephen?" an all-too-familiar voice asked.

They all turned to see Jake coming through the kitchen doorway.

"Saladin," Janey replied seriously.

"Not just Saladin," Lauren remarked, meaning the fed-up looking Janey.

Jake, however, chose to interpret her remark the wrong way.

"So you're missing Stephen, too, are you, Lauren?"

He gazed at her penetratingly for a moment, as if to say, but I thought we had such a good time together last Sunday. Lauren blushed.

"No," she said hastily, "I didn't mean me! I meant Janey."

"Ah, so all the women folk of Misty Towers are pining for our Doctor Dolittle, are they?" Jake asked sharply. "What about you, Daniel?" he asked the little boy. "Are you pining for Stephen, too?"

"Don't tease him," Lauren reproved Jake. "Was it Geoffrey you wanted?" she asked pointedly. "If so, I believe he's in his study."

"I came to see you, actually," Jake told her coolly, "to ask if you wanted to go to Corfe Castle for a pub lunch on Sunday. But I can sense my presence isn't welcome here, so I'll leave you in peace."

"Good riddance," Lauren retorted childishly.

"Ditto," Jake said, equally infantile, and he turned on his heel and left.

"Wow," a shocked Janey breathed, after

Jake had gone. "You sly old thing, Lauren. I didn't know you and Jake were an item. Whatever will Stephen say?" she teased.

Lauren felt the tell-tale blush rising again.

"Jake and I are not an item," she said firmly, busying herself with wiping Daniel's face. "I just went to an antiques fair with him once, that's all. And while we're about it, I might as well tell you that there's nothing going on between me and Stephen, either!"

That night, Lauren woke with a start. Heart pounding, she glanced across at her digital alarm clock. Quarter past two! Her little room was pitch dark. The house was silent. It must have been a bad dream that woke her. Shrugging, Lauren turned over and snuggled back down in the covers.

She was on the point of drifting back off to sleep when she heard it again, a thud. This time it was followed by a faint tinkling, like that of breaking glass. Lauren's heart started to pound, and a sense of misgiving pervaded her body. Could it be him? Could the burglar have returned again?

Suddenly fully awake, Lauren struggled upwards in the covers. Should she wake Geoffrey and Christine? But what if it wasn't an intruder at all, just a member of the family downstairs making themselves a drink, accidentally breaking a glass? Lauren would end up making a prize fool of herself, and no doubt irritating her employers into the bargain.

Mind you, she could creep down there and see for herself. Her heart lurched at the daring plan. The risks were all too obvious. If there was an intruder, he — or she — would possibly be armed, probably be dangerous. Legs swung over the edge of her bed, Lauren hesitated for a moment. Then she rose to pull on her discarded jeans and warm jumper. Then she stole across and turned the door handle, inching open her bedroom door. She peeped out on to the darkened landing. Silence. Stealthily, she tiptoed down the spiral staircase that led to the sitting-room.

Easing open the door that led to the sitting-room she stopped dead. Suddenly, all was pandemonium as an ear-splitting jangling filled the room. This time Geoffrey hadn't forgotten to set the alarm. From somewhere in the room there was a flurry of movement, a rustling and a chink of china or ceramic barely audible above the alarm. Then Lauren saw a figure, barely perceptible, dressed from head to toe in black, slowly turn in her direction.

A cold hand gripped Lauren's heart. She could hear voices and footsteps thudding on the stairs now but there was no time for hesitation. The next few moments passed in a flash. Suddenly the figure had disappeared back through the smashed French window. Lauren followed. Once outside, she couldn't see which way the intruder had gone, and by the time she spotted the figure once again making its way down the dark back garden towards the sea, the burglar had gained a couple of minutes on her.

Lauren paused anxiously, her breath coming in short raps. Then she spotted the tall, thin figure amongst the rhododendron bushes over to the west side of the garden. Panting, she scrambled after him, or her, just in time to see the figure disappear through a gap in the fence into Jake's garden! The burglar obviously knew the territory well. She pursued the shadowy figure out of Jake's garden and into the lane. Then a cloud passed across the moon and when, seconds later, the moon appeared again, she realised that the figure had gone.

Chapter Five

There was a knock at the door of Geoffrey Ferguson's study as he and Lauren sat expectantly.

"Ah," Geoffrey said, rising and going over to open it, "that'll be Jake."

It was indeed, looking slightly drawn in the early-morning light.

" 'Morning, Geoffrey, Lauren," Jake said soberly.

He turned to the police constable seated behind Geoffrey's desk.

"Good morning, Detective Inspector . . . er . . ."

"Barnes. Detective Constable Barnes," the little forty-something man replied, though clearly flattered by Jake's deliberate slip-up.

" 'Morning, Jake," Lauren managed.

When Lauren had returned to the house in the early hours, Geoffrey and Christine had already called the police, and when they arrived Lauren had undergone an extensive grilling. After a thorough search of the house Geoffrey had determined what was missing — a Japanese style jardinière and stand worth about ten thousand pounds. According to him, it was Jake who had acquired the antique for him and so, on the advice of the police, Geoffrey had phoned Jake at about half-past five that morning, asking him to come round immediately to give a full description of the item.

"I'd like to interview you in a moment if I may, Mr Rossiter," the policeman was saying now, "but first I would like to take Mr Ferguson to join my colleague at the crime scene so we can brush up on a few more details."

After the study door closed behind the other two men there was an awkward silence in the oak-panelled room. Then Jake spoke.

"I hear you had a bit of an adventure last night."

"That's not what I would call it," Lauren said indignantly, shivering at the memory. "How would you like to be a lone woman, alone on a heath in the dead of night with a potentially dangerous criminal?"

"I'm sorry," Jake replied, his voice regaining some of its usual warmth. "I didn't mean to sound insensitive."

"I should hope not," Lauren wavered. "It was quite traumatic, actually."

Suddenly the pent-up emotion of the encounter with the burglar was released, and Lauren began to cry quietly. Jake came over and put an awkward arm round her as she sat on the chair in front of Geoffrey's desk.

"Relax, Lauren," Jake said gently into her hair. "It's OK. You're safe now."

"But it's not OK!" she cried, wanting to believe his innocence but not daring to. "It could have been anyone up there on the heath last night. How do I know it wasn't you?"

Jake moved away, looking cross.

"And how do I know you weren't the criminal up there on the heath, and that this isn't all some elaborate story you've made up to divert suspicion?"

Lauren was almost speechless with indignance.

"But the burglar broke a window to get in. I wouldn't have needed to do that, would I?"

"You could have sct it up to look like that."

"That's a bit far-fetched, isn't it?" Lauren exclaimed angrily.

"No more so than you suspecting that I'm the thief," Jake fired back at her. "Geoffrey's my best friend, for goodness' sake, Lauren! And you — I thought you trusted me! What did this person look like anyway?" he demanded. "Did he even look anything like me?"

"It was dark, it was hard to tell," Lauren said defensively. "But, yes, from what I could see he was quite tall, and thin."

"Quite tall!" Jake echoed mockingly. "I'm six foot three! How much taller could you want? And thin! I know I'm not exactly overweight, but you could hardly call me a stick insect, could you?"

At that moment, the study door opened, and a serious-looking DC Barnes and a subdued-looking Geoffrey were standing on the threshold.

"Sorry, Geoffrey, DC Barnes," Lauren apologised meekly, her cheeks flaming.

She'd probably be their number one suspect after this debacle. Talk about a despicable character!

"Please, forgive me," she said humbly. "I didn't know you were there."

After they were finished with her, Lauren felt a little better after phoning her mother and chatting to her. Carole James was aghast.

"Calm down, Mum!" Lauren ordered. "I'm fine, I really am. And besides," she added, "I'll be seeing you all tomorrow, anyway."

Somehow Lauren was ready to tackle Daniel when he woke just before seven. She knew it was important that she treated the little boy as normally as possible, and acted as if this was just like any other day.

" 'Morning, Lauren, Daniel," Maggie Foster greeted them when they went down to the kitchen. "How are you now, Lauren?" Maggie asked, concerned, as Lauren strapped Daniel into the highchair.

She had obviously heard about the night's antics.

"Not too bad now, thanks, Maggie," Lauren replied.

The older woman was gazing sympathetically at her and Lauren felt the sudden urge to confide in someone.

"As if it wasn't bad enough being out on the heath at night alone with a criminal, I had to go and have a row with Jake afterwards. And then Geoffrey and the policeman walked in right when I was in mid-insult!"

There was a trace of a smile in Maggie's eyes.

"Funnily enough, I've just had Jake in here, telling me the same story."

Lauren began to feed Daniel.

"What?" Lauren gasped incredulously. "What a — a snitch."

Maggie shook her head gently.

"No, Lauren, Jake wasn't telling tales on you. He was telling me about your argument. The man was clearly upset about it, just as you are."

Lauren flushed again, feeling firmly put in her place.

"Jake's a good man, Lauren," Maggie was saying quietly. "And he thinks the world of you."

Lauren didn't know what to say to this. She felt overcome with guilt and shame that she may have suspected an innocent man. And all she could think was, if Jake wasn't the burglar, then who was? Suddenly, for no apparent reason, she thought of Stephen Hughes. He was the family vet, had been for a year. It would be despicable to betray their trust, and yet, suddenly, everything seemed to fit into place.

At that moment a jeans-clad Janey burst into the room.

"What a palaver!" she exclaimed in her

youthful, well-bred tones. "All that business last night. Poor mummy and daddy are in a right old state. Still, life goes on, I guess. This just arrived from Stephen."

She flung a postcard down on the kitchen table, with a night-time picture of Newcastle's famous bridge on its front.

"Feel free, Lauren, Maggie," Janey gestured towards it.

Lauren picked up the postcard and turned it over. It was addressed to the whole family, and postmarked the previous day. Lauren's heart suddenly felt as heavy as lead. Stephen Hughes was clearly in Newcastle. There was no way he could have committed the burglary. So where, she wondered painfully, did that leave Jake Rossiter.

After the drama of that Friday night and Saturday morning, the following week was something of an anti-climax. Lauren's parents were delighted to see her that Sunday, although Carole James was less than happy to let her daughter return to the house in Gorse Hill that evening.

"I always said no good would come of mixing with the folk of Gorse Hill," she muttered mysteriously.

"Mum," Lauren replied, fondly but exasperatedly, "either tell me what this is all about or shush."

With a pointed glance, Carole James chose to do the latter.

The long, school summer holiday had now arrived, and by late Monday morning Janey was beside herself with boredom.

"I can't bear it," she confided in Lauren in the kitchen. "Since the last burglary, Mummy and Daddy have kept me wrapped up in more cotton wool than ever. And I'm so far from any of my friends out here. I'm so bored."

"Leave it to me," Lauren told Janey, mysteriously.

That afternoon Lauren asked Christine what she thought about Lauren and Janey going to Ecclesdon's one and only night-club that Saturday. Christine frowned.

"I'm not so sure," she said anxiously. "I'm sorry, Lauren, but all this horrible business just makes one so over-protective. Although, hang on a minute," she said suddenly. "What about if Jake went with you? Janey's very fond of him. And Stephen's back from Newcastle tonight," Christine added. "He can make up the foursome. I'll get Geoffrey to give Jake a ring."

And so, before Lauren knew what was happening, she was condemned to an awkward evening with Jake, with whom she was still barely on speaking terms, with Janey and Stephen along to make it even more uncomfortable. Janey was delighted, of course.

"What do you think?" she asked, when Lauren arrived downstairs on the big night.

She pirouetted excitably, showing off an expensive-looking cream dress that fitted perfectly to her young figure.

"You look gorgeous, Janey," Lauren said truthfully.

"You look pretty fab, too," Janey enthused, gazing at Lauren.

Lauren glanced down uncertainly at her short black skirt and light blue halter-neck top. The doorbell rang, and moments later Maggie showed in Jake and Stephen. Both men looked good — Jake in a dark suit and Stephen in a smart shirt and chinos. She noticed Jake glance at her. He caught her eye, then they both looked away awkwardly.

There was a loud toot from outside.

"That'll be the taxi," Janey yelped excitedly. "Come on, let's go."

Stephen sat in the front of the taxi and Lauren sat in the back between Janey and Jake. As the driver revved up the engine Jake said in Lauren's ear, "Let's set aside our differences for tonight, shall we? And let's try and forget the unpleasant events of the last few days," Jake added. "Just try to enjoy the night."

Privately Lauren thought that the idea of enjoyment was highly unlikely that night, given her suspicions regarding both Jake and Stephen, but she kept her thoughts to herself. Once inside the darkened interior of the nightclub, Janey took one sip of her drink then grabbed Jake by the arm.

"Coming to dance, Jake?"

Jake, powerless to refuse, raised his eyebrows at Lauren as Janey dragged him towards the packed dance floor. Left alone with Stephen, Lauren was unable to resist saying, "I suppose you heard there was another burglary a week ago?"

"Yes, Christine told me about it, when I got back from Newcastle. I was at a vets' seminar. Did anyone tell you?"

"Yes, Janey mentioned it," Lauren said lightly.

"How about it, Lauren?" Stephen asked Lauren suddenly, gesturing towards the dance floor.

"OK," Lauren agreed.

Somehow they managed to find Jake and Janey amid the throng. She was unable to resist sneaking a glance at Jake. He and

Janey were dancing close together, too close for Lauren's liking, she realised with a shock. Hoping Jake was watching, Lauren moved a little closer to Stephen. Janey seemed to have boundless energy, and they all danced for five consecutive tracks before Jake made to leave.

"I can't hack the pace," he said. "Sorry, Janey. I need a drink."

Then he left, pushing his way between the heaving bodies. Janey joined Lauren and Stephen and they danced the next track together. Lauren realised she was having a great time, but as the song wore on she started to feel increasingly guilty about Jake.

"I'd better go and see where Jake is," she shouted.

Leaving the other two on the floor, she found Jake at the bar.

"Hi," she said cautiously, pulling up a bar-stool beside him.

"Hi," Jake replied. "It's OK. Go back to the dance floor."

"It's all right," Lauren told him. "I needed a breather anyway."

"Can I get you a drink?"

"I think I'll have just a soft drink this time, thanks," she said. "You seemed to be having a pretty good time with Janey just now."

"Likewise with you and Stephen," Jake retorted smoothly.

"How many times do I have to tell you, Jake, we are just friends."

"Ah," Jake remarked, sipping his drink. "That hoary old chestnut, just friends. And to think," he went on, one eyebrow raised, "I was taken in that time you came to my house and told me you liked me. More fool me."

Lauren grimaced at the memory of that deceitful afternoon.

"It's true, though," she said, forcing the words out. "I do like you. I just happen to like Stephen, too."

"Ah, speak of the devil," a scowling Jake interrupted her.

Swivelling round on her stool, Lauren saw Stephen and Janey approaching. There was a look of thunder in Stephen's dark blue eyes.

"There you are, Lauren!" he exclaimed crossly. "I thought you'd be coming back to join us."

He grabbed a bar-stool next to Lauren.

"So, anyway, Lauren," Stephen said, leaning a little closer to her, with a smile, "let's fix a date for that long-awaited sailing trip, shall we?"

"Oh!" Lauren exclaimed, surprised, with

a sideways glance at Jake, who was glowering darkly. "I thought you'd forgotten about that."

"Of course not! I never break a promise," Stephen said extravagantly, taking a draught from his pint of lager. "How about next weekend?"

Suddenly Lauren wasn't at all sure she wanted to go on a date with Stephen, and it wasn't just because Jake was sitting next to her with a face like a storm cloud. She just wasn't attracted to Stephen. The simple truth was that she preferred Jake.

"What's the matter, Lauren?" Jake said suddenly. "Cat got your tongue? Or are you simply speechless with excitement at the thought of a date with Doctor Dolittle?"

Right, that did it! Turning to Stephen, Lauren said, "It would have to be Sunday. That's my day off."

Stephen beamed.

"It's Sunday tomorrow, and the forecast is fine with a bit of a breeze, just right for sailing. So, have you made any other plans or are you free?"

"Er, no," she said slowly.

"Right, tomorrow it is, then."

Stephen seemed to give a triumphant glance at Jake.

"Another drink, Lauren? Same again, or

something a little stronger?"

While Stephen was ordering the drinks, Jake turned to her.

"So," he said, "you still maintain that Hughes means nothing to you?"

"Nothing more than a friend," Lauren said curtly.

"So why did you just agree to go on a date with him tomorrow?"

To needle you, was the truthful answer, but Lauren just said, "Because I felt obligated, as we'd previously arranged it."

The mood on the dance floor changed then, as the disc jockey played a slow track. Suddenly a different look entered Jake's eyes.

"If Hughes means nothing to you," he challenged Lauren, "dance this one with me."

Lauren's eyes widened and she gazed at Jake in alarm. She was loathe to get into close proximity to Jake again, after what had happened when they had been in each other's arms the last couple of times. But if she refused, Jake would claim she was lying about her feelings for Stephen.

"OK," Lauren said, reluctantly, but she couldn't help a traitorous thrill of excitement as Jake led her to the dance floor.

On the floor, however, it seemed the

most natural thing in the world to relax into Jake's arms. Jake raised a hand to smooth her shoulder and she was unable to stop herself from raising her face to his. The next minute he was kissing her full on the mouth, and Lauren was kissing him back.

Finally she pulled away from him, confused. Then Lauren fled, stumbling through a maze of dancers, half-blinded by tears.

Chapter Six

Stephen had been right. The following morning dawned bright and sunny, with the hint of a breeze. Lauren rose at eight and dressed without enthusiasm in shorts and a fitted top. Her head was aching.

She stumbled blearily into the kitchen.

"Oh, 'morning, Maggie, Derek."

Lauren was surprised to see not only Maggie seated at the scrubbed pine table, but her husband, too. Lauren hadn't seen that much of Derek since she'd come to work at Misty Towers, as he spent most of his time outdoors, but he seemed a very nice man. Both Maggie and Derek were nursing mugs of tea, and there was an unexpected air of solemnity in the room. Lauren's expression grew concerned.

"Is something up?"

"You tell Lauren," Maggie told Derek, rising. "Sit down, Lauren. I'll get you some tea."

"It's not a matter of life and death," Derek told Lauren, his shrewd, intelligent grey eyes gazing at her anxious face with concern. "It's just that Mr Ferguson called Maggie and me into his study to have a word with him yesterday, and told us that financial circumstances are going to force him to give us a substantial pay cut."

Lauren was full of indignance on the couple's behalf.

"What? And this was the first you knew of it?"

"Oh, no," Derek sighed ruefully. "Geoffrey did warn me a few weeks ago that things were getting a little tight financially and that something like this would probably happen."

"I can't believe it. Talk about gratitude!" Lauren said exasperatedly. "How long have you worked for the Fergusons? Ten years, is it?"

Derek nodded, lines of anxiety clearly etched on his face.

"They'd almost likely cut your wages, too, Lauren," he told her, "but you're probably on too much of a pittance to start with. I suppose it's not Geoffrey's fault," he reasoned. "It's just that things are a little tight financially for Maggie and me, too, right now."

Maggie handed Lauren her tea, then stood beside her husband, putting a comforting hand on his shoulder.

"Our eldest, Stephanie, is getting married at Christmas," Maggie explained, "and we've promised her a big white wedding. Plus we're helping our Simon out with his mortgage repayments, too."

"All in all," Derek said sadly, "everything's turned into one gigantic mess."

Lauren was too concerned for Maggie and Derek to worry what this might mean regarding her own wages. Anyway, like Derek said, if they cut her wages she'd be earning thin air.

"I'm so sorry, I don't know what to say."

"Penny for them?" Stephen called across to Lauren, as she sat on the deck of the yacht, gazing absently at the passing waves.

"What? Oh."

Lauren looked up guiltily, aware that Stephen was doing all the work of sailing the yacht.

"Sorry," she called back.

"What's wrong? Aren't you enjoying yourself? Sure you aren't more of a land-lubber at heart?" he asked, on a teasing note.

Lauren forced a smile.

"No, I've practically got salt water coursing through my veins! I'm having a great time."

It should have been true. Stephen had planned the day meticulously, driving her down to the beach at Gorse Hill, then rowing her out in a little dinghy to where his yacht, Guillemot, was moored in the bay.

"We'll sail over to Poole," he'd told her, "then stop for a spot of lunch."

Lauren had smiled her agreement, while all the time her mind was preoccupied with more disturbing thoughts. Now they were sailing along, the white sails billowing in the wind. She had to admit that the coastline was spectacular from this vantage point, especially as Poole loomed into view, the second largest natural harbour in the world.

"Right, I'll just moor her up here," Stephen called. "You can help if you like, Lauren, if you think you're up to it."

"Of course. Just tell me what to do."

Moments later, the job was accomplished, and the boat was bobbing gently in the waters of Poole Harbour.

"This is nice," Stephen said, sighing with satisfaction. "I'll fetch the picnic in a minute. D'you want to go down and freshen up first?"

"Oh, yes, thanks."

Rather uncertainly, Lauren descended the steps to the lower deck. Her head was still feeling fuzzy with the remains of a hangover. Had Stephen said it was the first cabin door or the second? Lauren picked the second door. As soon as she opened it, however, she realised her mistake. It was clearly a bedroom and, intrigued, she couldn't help gazing around the tiny cabin with interest.

"Are you OK down there?" Stephen called out, making her jump.

"Yes, fine," Lauren called back.

She was moving to close the cabin door when she gave a low gasp of pain. Bending down to see what she'd caught her shin on, she saw a long, cardboard box sticking out slightly from under the bed. Instinct made her lift the flap of the box and peep inside, and what she saw made her gasp again. Swathed in tissue paper was a Japanese-style jardinière!

Head spinning, Lauren knew she had to move quickly, or Stephen would grow suspicious and come down to check up on her. His Newcastle alibi remained a mystery at present. Rather unsteadily, Lauren climbed back up into the brightness on deck, where Stephen was lounging as if he hadn't a care in the world.

"OK?" he asked with a smile.

"Fine, thanks," Lauren replied, trying to make her voice sound normal.

It wasn't easy, given the realisation that she was trapped alone on a yacht with the thief. Did he suspect that she knew? If so, heaven only knew what he might do to her.

"What about that picnic?" she asked nervously. "I'm so hungry I could eat a horse."

"The picnic can wait," Stephen said suddenly, leaning towards her.

Lauren realised then that he was going to kiss her. She didn't know whether to be relieved or horrified. Gently Stephen clasped her wrist.

"Lauren," Stephen was murmuring, "I've wanted to do this for so long."

As his lips brushed hers, Lauren pulled away sharply, heart pounding.

"No!" she shrieked.

Stephen pulled back, clearly shocked.

"Hey, steady on!" he exclaimed. "What's the matter?"

Somehow, Lauren managed to calm herself.

"The time's not right," she murmured hastily. "It — it's too soon."

Her thoughts were racing frantically, as she tried to work out how she was going to get off this godforsaken yacht. Stephen Hughes was potentially a very dangerous man, she realised, and yet in the midst of her fear, another realisation had come unbidden. Even if Stephen had been innocent, Lauren would not have wanted him to kiss her, because, like it or not, she had to face the fact that she had fallen in love with Jake.

Somehow Lauren persuaded Stephen to take her back to the beach at Gorse Hill, feigning seasickness. After dropping her off he took the dinghy back to the yacht, claiming there was some work he wanted to do on board.

Lauren stumbled back up the gently-sloping hill from the beach, her head in a spin. She had to get back to the house fast, and tell Geoffrey and Christine what had been going on. Hopefully they'd be able to get to the yacht in time to catch Stephen red-handed.

Finally she arrived back at Misty Towers, exhausted and trembling, feeling as if her lungs would burst.

"Afternoon, Lauren," Jake said curtly from the Fergusons' front steps.

Lauren jumped. Even in an emergency,

her newly-discovered feelings for the man made her unable to meet his eye.

"Afternoon, Jake," she replied, her words almost falling over themselves. "I'm afraid I can't stop. I've got to speak to Christine and Geoffrey, urgently."

Jake raised his dark eyebrows at this.

"Well, it looks like, urgent or not, you'll have to wait. I called round for a word with Geoff, and Janey told me she'd just had a phone call from her parents. They'd gone out for the day with Daniel, over to Lyme Regis, to try and forget about the burglaries and everything. But the car's broken down, and they don't expect to be back until this evening."

"Oh, no!" Lauren cried, dismayed.

"What's up, Lauren?" he asked. "Did your date with Stephen go OK?"

"For the last time, Jake," Lauren burst out exasperatedly, "it wasn't a date. And no," she added, more subdued, "it didn't go OK."

"Bit of a disappointment, was it?" Jake asked caustically. "Don't tell me, it wasn't a yacht, it was a dinghy after all."

"Why do you always have to trivialise everything, Jake? Maybe it was something more serious than what sort of boat Stephen's got."

Instantly, Jake's mood changed.

"What do you mean, Lauren?" he asked sharply. "Hughes didn't do something to upset you, did he?"

For a moment, Lauren was so tempted to confide in Jake what she knew. She gazed at him for a long minute, on the brink of unburdening her heart. Then she thought better of it.

The Fergusons would be home soon, and it was best that she told them first. Jake was the last person she felt like confiding in right now.

A look of hurt flashed through Jake's eyes, then they darkened again.

"Very well. I won't force you to talk about it if you don't wish to. Goodbye, Lauren," he said abruptly, then he was off.

Lauren paced restlessly around her room for the rest of that afternoon, ears strained for the sound of Geoffrey Ferguson's key in the front door. But all remained quiet downstairs. Maggie had clearly decided to take herself off for the day, even Janey had retreated to her bedroom to listen to music.

At about seven, Lauren supposed she ought to eat something, and padded down to the kitchen to make herself an omelette. She ate it listlessly. Suddenly the door creaked open, causing Lauren almost to jump out of her skin.

"What do you want?" she exclaimed, seeing Jake in the doorway.

"I was concerned about you," Jake said gruffly.

There was a moment's awkwardness as they looked at each other, as if both were remembering the way they had held each other and kissed only the night before. It seemed like a lifetime ago. He came into the room.

"You seemed anxious about something earlier, and I felt uneasy, seeing we'd parted on bad terms."

"Bad terms?" Lauren scoffed, setting down her knife and fork. "By our standards, we were getting on like a house on fire just then."

The corners of Jake's mouth lifted in what was almost a smile.

"So," he asked, coming to sit down opposite her at the scrubbed pine table, "do I take it that Geoff and Chrissie still aren't home?"

"Got it in one," Lauren nodded.

Once again, Jake's large, comforting presence was tempting her, despite their differences, to confide in him, to tell him everything. But she knew she mustn't.

Abruptly she scraped back her chair.

"Do you want a cup of tea?" she asked, getting to her feet.

If she busied herself, she wouldn't be so tempted to talk.

"I wouldn't say no," Jake replied.

There was another sound at the doorway, and both Lauren and Jake spun round to see the newcomer. There was an air of nervous anticipation in the room. But it wasn't Geoffrey and Christine, just Janey.

Janey looked briefly surprised to see Lauren and Jake sitting there.

"Hi, Lauren, hi, Jake," she murmured, going over to the fridge and taking out a carton of orange juice.

She was about to slurp some straight from the carton, then clearly thought better of it and fetched herself a glass. Lauren couldn't help watching as Janey slopped some juice on to the work surface.

"Damn!" Janey exclaimed irritably, then lapsed back into silence.

"Are you OK, Janey?" Lauren asked.

"Not really," Janey muttered in reply.

"What's up?" Jake asked, sounding concerned.

Janey leaned against the work surface.

"I'm just so bored. I've been cooped up here all day on my own. My friend,

Amanda, rang earlier, said a group of them are going out to a pub in Wareham tonight. I think I might just slip off and join them."

"I don't think that would be such a good idea," Lauren said slowly.

"I agree with Lauren," Jake said.

Lauren flashed him a grateful glance.

"It wouldn't be a good idea at all."

To Lauren's surprise, Janey started to nod in agreement.

"And Mummy and Daddy would go ballistic if I wasn't in when they finally returned from the back of beyond. Yes, Lauren, Jake," she said wearily, "I suppose you're both right."

Then she set down her glass on the work surface and left.

When Janey had gone, Jake said, "Poor kid."

"Mmm," Lauren agreed. "Thanks for supporting me there, by the way."

Jake grinned across at her, in a way that turned her heart over.

"Any time," he told her. "For a moment there I almost felt as if we were the middle-aged parents of a stroppy adolescent."

Lauren flushed. Jake was implying that they were like a comfortable, established couple, bonded by years of shared experiences and love.

"So," he continued, "would you like me to stay, keep you company till Geoff and Chrissie get back?"

For a moment Lauren was tempted to say, yes, but this was too cosy, too comfortable. Any minute now she'd be unburdening her heart to Jake, which was the last thing she should do.

"No," she said, her tone cooling once again. "No, thank you, Jake. I'll be fine on my own."

When Jake had gone, Lauren returned to her room where she tried to immerse herself in a novel, all the while listening out for the sound of the Fergusons' return. It was midnight when she finally admitted defeat and went to bed. She doubted she'd sleep anyway, with her mind racing so. As soon as she heard the front door she would leap out of bed and go and tell Geoffrey and Christine of her unsettling discovery.

Surprisingly, Lauren was almost drifting off when she heard a noise downstairs. Immediately she sat bolt upright in bed, straining her ears. She was reminded of the other night. Could it be another burglary? she thought in sudden fear. No, she reassured herself firmly. It was far more likely to be a weary Geoffrey, Christine and

Daniel arriving home from their epic day out.

She pulled on her faded old jeans and deep-blue sweater. Then she clattered quickly down the spiral stone staircase. Hearing another noise coming from the front hall, she crossed the darkened sitting-room hastily.

Suddenly the phone at the far end of the sitting-room rang, jangling into the silence. In her state of heightened tension, Lauren froze, waiting for Geoffrey or Christine, if it was them, to come in and answer the phone. But the phone rang again, and again. A horrible thought struck Lauren. Maybe the presence in the hall was the burglar. Stephen!

On trembling legs, Lauren ran over to the table at the end of the room and snatched up the receiver.

"Hello?" she asked nervously.

"Oh, Lauren, hello, it's Christine here."

At the sound of Christine Ferguson's familiar, friendly voice echoing down the phone line, Lauren's heart lurched ominously. If Christine and Geoffrey weren't out there in the hall, then who was?

Chapter Seven

"Christine?" Lauren stammered in reply, glancing towards the door that led to the hallway. "But I thought . . ."

"I do apologise for waking you, Lauren," Christine was saying. "I thought Janey would answer the phone. I've been ringing her on my mobile, keeping her posted."

Trust Janey not to have mentioned this, Lauren thought incongruously.

"Anyway," Christine went on, "just to let you know that we're almost home. It took longer to fix the car than we thought, and then the traffic was horrendous. We should have stayed the night in a hotel, really, but we wanted to get home to Janey. I suppose she must be asleep now."

"I suppose so," Lauren echoed, robot-like.

"Anyway, you go back to bed, Lauren. We'll see you in the morning."

"Actually," Lauren began desperately, "there was something . . ."

But it was too late. Christine had rung off. Lauren strained her ears. All was silent. Maybe she had imagined the sounds in the hall. Then as Lauren put the phone down, she heard a door slam — the front door! Her heart began to pound. It couldn't be Geoffrey and Christine coming in. They wouldn't have got here already, and then it struck her — it might not be someone coming in, it might be Janey leaving. Lauren rushed across and flung open the hall door.

The hallway was empty. Lauren pulled open the heavy front door and peered out into the night. She heard a crunch of gravel, and then, sure enough, glimpsed Janey, dressed in jeans and a leather jacket, carrying a shoulder bag, disappearing off down the hill. Janey had chosen to defy her and Jake, and sneak off to meet her friends in Wareham after all.

Instinct led Lauren up the hill, to Jake's house. She stumbled up his steps and hammered urgently on his front door. The door opened and Jake stood there illuminated in the light from his hall, looking slightly bleary-eyed but still dressed in jeans and a black shirt.

"Oh," Lauren gabbled in relief, "you haven't gone to bed yet!"

"No," Jake agreed bemusedly, looking at her. "I couldn't sleep anyway. I was watching a late film. What is it, Lauren? What do you want?"

"It's Janey!" Lauren gasped. "She's sneaked off to meet her friend, Amanda. I thought that maybe if we took your car, we might catch her."

Instantly Jake's manner became businesslike as he pulled the door shut and raced over to where his car was parked in the drive.

"Climb in," he said briskly.

Within seconds they were belted up and he was revving the engine.

They roared off down the hill. They were halfway down the hill that gave Gorse Hill its name when Lauren cried out.

"I can see her — look! About a hundred yards ahead."

Janey was standing at the roadside with her bag at her feet, and seemed to be waiting for someone.

"Hang on a minute," Jake said, slowing the car. "There's a car coming up the hill."

Jake pulled over, parking his car in the shadows. The other car pulled up beside Janey, and as it did so, Lauren could see by the nearby streetlamp that it was a dark green Range Rover.

"That's Stephen's car!" she exclaimed breathlessly, her heart thudding in sudden alarm. "What's Janey doing, getting in Stephen's car?"

"I don't know," Jake whispered back. "Let's watch and find out."

As they watched, Stephen emerged from the car and embraced Janey. Lauren watched, dumbstruck, as the two kissed.

"I don't believe it," Lauren breathed. "Janey and Stephen are an item!"

She flushed, recalling how she'd believed Stephen was interested in her, and had pretended Janey was nothing more than an irritating schoolgirl.

"Looks pretty much like it."

Jake sounded equally stunned. They watched as Stephen took Janey's bag from her, flung it into the back of the car, and opened the passenger door for her to get in.

"So that story about meeting her friends in Wareham was just a cover," Lauren said incredulously.

Jake nodded.

"And she must have arranged for Stephen to pick her up out of sight of the house."

"This might not be the most opportune

moment to break this to you," Lauren told Jake quickly, "but when I was on Stephen's yacht today, I discovered Geoffrey's stolen Japanese urn thing."

"Jardinière," Jake corrected. "You mean, Stephen Hughes has got it? You're saying Hughes is the burglar?"

"Looks like it."

"And does Hughes know that you know?"

"Maybe. I'm not sure."

"Why didn't you tell me all this earlier this afternoon?" Jake demanded. "I knew something was up with you. I kept asking you what the matter was!"

"It didn't seem right. I thought Geoffrey and Christine should know first."

As Lauren spoke, her reasoning sounded pretty pathetic to her.

"And they still hadn't got home by midnight, so I went to bed. Then Christine rang to say they were on their way. They should be passing through Corfe Castle about now."

"Hey, they're driving off!"

Jake jerked his head towards the Range Rover, then quickly revved up his car, roaring off in pursuit. They trailed the Range Rover down to the bottom of the hill and into the village, continuing down towards the beach.

"Where are they going?" Lauren whispered.

"I'll give you three guesses," Jake growled in reply.

He pulled the car over to the side of the winding country road, extracting his mobile phone from his pocket. Rapidly he punched in a number.

"Dave? It's Jake. Look, I'm really sorry to disturb you at this time of night, but it's an emergency. Can I borrow the boat? Great. I owe you one. I'll explain later. As I said, it's an emergency. Thanks a lot, mate. 'Bye."

"What's going on, Jake?" Lauren asked warily.

"Don't worry, Laurie," Jake replied tersely. "I've got the matter in hand."

"Don't you think you'd better phone the police?" she asked.

He punched out some more digits.

"Police, please . . . Hello. Yes, I'm at the east side of Gorse Hill beach. There's a potentially armed robber, possible kidnapper of a seventeen-year-old girl, attempting to make an escape, probably by yacht. Great. 'Bye."

Shoving the phone back into his jeans pocket, Jake swerved the car back into the road and roared off into the night. He rounded the corner into the beach carpark. It was deserted, but for one other car — a dark green Range Rover. There was no sign of its occupants.

"Come on," Jake ordered, leaping out of the car. "Stay close to me," he told her. "And don't try any heroics."

"Why not?" Lauren asked indignantly. "It's thanks to me that we're on Stephen's trail in the first place."

"Because you mean a lot to me," Jake told her firmly, "and I don't want anything happening to you. I'm too selfish. Now come on."

He ran off down the muddy track that led to the beach and Lauren followed him mechanically. Her mind was in a daze. Jake had said she meant a lot to him. Could that mean he was in love with her? But she couldn't think about that now. She must focus her attention on the present.

Jake made for one of the wooden beach huts that faced out of the surrounding woodland on to the beach, scrabbling in the sand under the wooden decking and producing a key.

"This way," he told Lauren, running across the sand to where a small, wooden jetty extended into the sea and a sleekly-curved white speedboat was moored, moving gently with the waves.

"Here," he said, jumping in.

He held out his hand for Lauren to grasp, swinging her easily down into the bobbing boat.

"Look!" Jake said, pointing. "That yacht over there's setting sail."

Lauren strained her eyes in the darkness.

"Yes, and it looks like Stephen's yacht. I don't think they've seen us yet."

"Well, let's go," Jake said urgently, loosening the boat's moorings.

Suddenly they were roaring through the waves.

"Do you think they've seen us?" Lauren shouted above the roar.

"They have now," Jake said grimly.

Sure enough, Lauren could make out Stephen's life-jacketed figure on board the yacht, head turned in their direction. There was another figure beside him — Janey. The sea spray was wet on Lauren's face.

"Hey!" she cried suddenly. "There's another boat!"

"Stop! Police!" a tinny voice came through a loud-hailer.

The coastguard's boat had appeared from out of the night and was approaching Stephen's yacht from the opposite direction, heading it off. Suddenly the sky was filled with the thudding sound of a helicopter. As the sound became louder Lauren glanced up to see a blinding light.

"The police helicopter!" she exclaimed incredulously. "Wow, they've really pulled all the stops out, haven't they?"

"It's a serious matter," Jake told her. "Janey's a vulnerable, young female, practically a minor. She's safe now, thank God," Jake added with feeling.

It seemed like only seconds later they were all assembled on the wooden jetty — Lauren, Jake, Stephen, Janey, two policemen and a policewoman. One of the policemen had phoned Janey's parents, who were now on their way over. The policewoman was comforting Janey.

The older of the two policemen, a plump, balding man, was saying to Stephen, "Stephen Hughes, we are arresting you on suspicion of robbery and attempted kidnap."

Suddenly Janey interrupted, breaking free from the policewoman.

"Stephen's not a kidnapper! I was going with him of my own free will. We were going to sail to France together, to start a new life. He's not a thief for that matter, either. I am."

Jake said, "You mean, you stole those antiques from your own parents?"

"Yes."

Janey nodded. In the moonlight her cropped hair gave her a mischievous, urchin look. The half-light silhouetted her figure, fairly tall, slim and in that instant, Lauren knew it was Janey she had followed on the heath that night.

"What's the big deal?" Janey went on. "It was all going to be mine one day, anyway. I was just speeding up the process."

"You were leaving to start a new life together?" Jake repeated.

"That's right."

For the first time, Stephen spoke.

"I'm madly in love with Janey and I think she feels the same about me. But we knew her parents would never approve of our relationship."

Lauren frowned.

"Why not?"

Stephen laughed mirthlessly.

"Oh, come on. Janey's their golden girl, the apple of her daddy's eye. I'm a twenty-eight-year-old divorcé. There was no way they were going to endorse our engagement. So we decided to run away to Europe together."

"It was my idea," Janey put in defensively. "Stephen didn't want anything to do with it at first, but I talked him into it. We didn't have much money of our own, so I stole the antiques, planning to sell them on."

Stephen turned to Lauren.

"I'm sorry I misled you about the nature of my feelings towards you, Lauren. But Janey and I agreed I had to do it, in order to distract attention away from Janey and myself."

Jake glanced at her, and Lauren flushed at the memory of how she had been deceived by Stephen's attentions.

"Apology accepted," she said curtly.

The balding policeman turned to Janey.

"So, Miss Ferguson," he asked in his brisk, interrogative manner, "you claim you were responsible for stealing the antiques?"

"That's right," Janey confirmed. "The silver card-case was easy enough, so small, I just slipped it into my pocket. The timing was all-important. I stole the card-case the night after Lauren, Miss James, had been to the house for her interview. Sorry, Lauren, but I figured that one extra suspect would help distract from Stephen and me. But the card-case didn't fetch much, only three hundred pounds. I realised I'd have to go on to bigger and better things. Then one night, the night of your welcoming dinner party, Lauren, I overheard Daddy and Jake discussing the green vase by the picture window. Jake told Daddy the vase was worth three thousand pounds, so I decided that I would steal it that night."

"Fortunately for you, your father had forgotten to set the burglar alarm," Lauren commented.

Janey's betrayal hurt her. It was as if she had been betrayed by a friend.

"That was fortunate, yes. But if I'd needed to, I could easily have turned the alarm off. Mummy and Daddy showed me how," Janey gloated.

"So that just leaves us with the theft of the third item," the second, younger policeman said coaxingly. "The Japanese-style jardinière."

"Well," Janey said, "we knew we needed a lot more money, and that time was running out. So we decided to go for one final big one. I remembered Daddy crowing, some time ago, when Jake sold him that jardinière for eight thousand pounds. Jake told Daddy it was likely to fetch nearer ten thousand at auction. At the time I wasn't so sure. You're a lovely chap, Jake, but I couldn't help wondering if you were fleecing poor Daddy."

"Excuse me!" Jake burst out indignantly.

139

"Don't tar everyone with your own brush, Janey. Just because I'm an astute businessman doesn't mean I'm a crook. And I'd certainly never cheat my best friend!"

Janey looked chastened at this, but she went on.

"We were worried people were starting to suspect Stephen, so we timed this burglary while he was away at that seminar in Newcastle. We even arranged for him to send a postcard back, for good measure."

"Only, this time," Lauren interposed, "your father did set the alarm."

"That's right," Janey agreed. "So I had to unset it while I put the jardinière into my holdall. Then I went outside and smashed the French window, so that it would really look as if an intruder had broken in. After that, I reset the alarm, deliberately setting it off. It was at that point that I saw you, Lauren, and knew that things hadn't gone quite to plan. I realised then that I would have to make a quick getaway."

"Miss James," the balding policeman interrupted, referring to his notepad, where he had earlier written Lauren's name, "you say that when you were on board Mr Hughes' yacht, in the early afternoon of yesterday, you saw one of the stolen antiques, a Japanese-style jardinière, which one of our officers has recently recovered from the aforementioned yacht."

"That's right," Lauren confirmed.

"I knew you'd seen it," Stephen burst out, with a trace of bitterness. "You'd left the box sticking out from under the bed. That's why I decided Janey and I must leave tonight."

"So, Mr Hughes," the policeman spoke again, "could you enlighten us as to the whereabouts of the rest of the stolen antiques?"

"They've already been sold," Stephen confirmed shamefully. "I can provide receipts, of course. We didn't really have anywhere to hide the antiques, and besides, we needed the money. Needless to say, I feel dreadful about it all now."

"So do I," Janey said, looking suddenly repentant. "All I can say, Lauren, Jake, is that we're both terribly sorry."

"It's not us you should be apologising to," Jake said gruffly.

"No," Lauren added seriously, looking straight at Janey. "You should save it for your parents."

"Mummy and Daddy? They wouldn't understand. They've never really cared about me. Oh, yes, they cosset and protect me, but they don't really care about what's best for me. So much fuss about their precious possessions. They care more about those antiques than they do about me."

Lauren exchanged glances with Jake. She didn't really think that what Janey said was true. She sincerely hoped it wasn't, but the real tragedy was that Janey believed it was.

Soon after a shattered-looking Geoffrey and Christine turned up, Lauren and Jake were allowed to return to their car to drive home. Policemen would be visiting them in a short while at home, they were told, to take down their formal statements. By this time, it was nearly five in the morning, and the sun was beginning to rise. As the two of them walked back up the muddy track to Jake's car, Lauren turned guiltily to him.

"Jake?" she began nervously.

"Yes?"

"I'm sorry that I suspected you to begin with."

Jake feigned surprise.

"What? You mean to say that you suspected me?"

"Yes," Lauren muttered. "And I'm sure you were aware of the fact."

"Of course I was," Jake said matter-of-factly. "But, honestly, Lauren, do you really think I would have been that stupid, to

142

have stolen from my neighbour and best friend? But it's OK, you needn't apologise."

"Why not?"

"Because, as a matter of fact, I suspected you, too, at first."

"You did? Why?"

"Because the burglaries seemed to coincide with when you came to the house, for one thing, and after the second burglary, I knew it must be an insider, because although the culprit had broken the glass from the inside, so that it looked like they'd broken out, they had broken the pane too far away for them to have actually been able to reach the window handle."

Though impressed by this deduction, Lauren couldn't help being surprised at having been the focus of Jake's suspicion.

"Thanks a lot for suspecting me."

They were nearly back at Jake's car now. He turned to her.

"I didn't really suspect you, in particular, Lauren. As I think I told you at the time, I was just keeping an open mind."

"As I should have done, I know," Lauren said shamefully, as Jake unlocked the car. "Still, Janey and Stephen. I still can't get over it."

"Me neither. Anyway," he went on, as he

held the door open for her, "you've had one heck of a night, Lauren. If you tell me where your parents live, I'll drop you back home, and you can have a bath or whatever and then catch up on some sleep. I'll explain to the Fergusons where you are."

"Thanks, Jake," she said sincerely.

Jake frowned, as if in sudden remembrance.

"Your parents are away at the moment, aren't they? Scotland, wasn't it?"

"That's right."

"Are you sure you'll be OK on your own in the house, then?" Jake asked, his expression concerned. "You can come and sleep in my guest room if you like, phone your folks from my house."

For a moment, Lauren was sorely tempted by the comfort and reassurance of Jake's company. But it was best that she went home first, got herself sorted out.

"I'll be fine, thanks. My brothers will be at home anyway, so it won't be as if I'm going back to an empty house."

Once they were both sitting inside the car, Lauren steeled herself to ask Jake something she had been wanting to for a while. She now knew she was in love with him. She just had to find out if he felt the same about her.

"You know when we were at the beach, Jake, and you told me I meant a lot to you?"

"Yes?"

Lauren's cheeks reddened, as she lowered her gaze slightly.

"Did you really mean it?"

He reached out his large hand to cover her small, paler one.

"Of course I did, Lauren."

At his words, Lauren's heart began to beat faster and her body felt flushed with heat.

"Our relationship may have got off to a tempestuous start, but over the weeks I think it's deepened into a really strong friendship."

Suddenly all the colour drained from Lauren's face.

"Friendship?" she echoed, in a small voice.

"That's right."

Somehow, Lauren forced a smile, though inside it felt as if her heart was breaking.

"Oh, great," she managed to say.

But her disappointment was bitter. When Jake had said she meant a lot to him, he had meant as a friend. Yet at the time she had taken his words to mean so much more. Once again, Jake the charmer had deceived her with his smooth-flowing, empty words. Jake had been playing fast and loose with her heart.

Chapter Eight

Lauren had hardly had time to explain everything to her incredulous twin brothers when the police turned up.

"And after you've talked to the police, Laurie," Michael ordered her, "you're to phone Mum and Dad. Mum would never forgive you, or me, for that matter, if you didn't let her know all that has happened."

"But you know what Mum's like!" Lauren protested. "She'd insist on coming home straight away. I don't want to ruin their holiday."

"No buts, Laurie," Michael said. "You're ringing her, and that's final."

Any further protests Lauren might have made were cut short by the entrance of the two policemen from the beach.

"Hello again, Miss James," the plump, balding half of the duo said. "Now if you don't mind, we'd just like to go over things one more time."

Just as Lauren and her brother had expected, their mother insisted on returning home right away. It was almost eleven o'clock that night by the time they got back from Scotland, tired, and the boys had gone to bed. Lauren recounted the full story.

When Lauren finished, Carole James sighed and said, "I can't believe all that has happened to my biggest baby. I just feel so guilty. I shouldn't have let you go back to that place when all this funny business started."

"Don't be silly, Mum," Lauren said firmly. "There's no need to feel guilty. I wouldn't have let you keep me away from Misty Towers if you'd tried."

"Still," Carole went on, "no good ever came to our family from the folk of Gorse Hill."

"Mum," Lauren said determinedly, "I think it's time you told me exactly what happened to my great-grandma."

"Go on, love," her father said. "I think Laurie ought to know the truth. I'm bushed. I think I'll turn in."

Paul James left the room quietly.

"Well, Lauren," Carole began slowly,

"your great-grandmother, Violet, as I've told you before, once worked in a big house on Gorse Hill, as a housemaid. She was only nineteen. As you've probably seen from the old photos, Violet was a very pretty young woman. The thing is, the twenty-year-old son of the house, William, fell madly in love with Violet, and she felt the same about him. Only, when the boy's father found out, he was furious, said there was no way William was marrying below his station. So poor Violet was sacked. She was devastated. Of course, we all know she eventually married your great-grandfather, George, and was happy enough, but she never really recovered from that first, doomed love affair. It wasn't until just before she died that she told the whole story to your granny."

"So Granny told you all about it?"

Carole James nodded. Lauren thought of her much-loved granny, alive and well and living in a luxury retirement flat in Poole.

"She told me to tell you about it when I thought you were old enough."

"I guess that must mean you finally think I'm grown up, Mum."

Her mother smiled back.

"You've been a mature young woman for years, Laurie. I'm the one who didn't want to accept that my baby had grown up. So? How do you feel, now that you know the truth?"

"It's a very poignant story," she told her mother, "and I'll never forget it, but it won't change my feelings towards the Fergusons. Geoffrey and Christine have treated me with nothing but kindness, and just because they're well-off and from Gorse Hill, it doesn't mean they're bad people. What's past is past," Lauren added.

"There's just one more thing," Lauren began, with a sudden twinge of anxiety. "What was the name of the house my great-granny worked in?"

"Godlingston House," Carole James replied, adding curiously, "Why?"

"Oh, I just thought I might take a walk there tomorrow, lay a few ghosts."

And maybe if she walked past Jake's house, she could lay the ghosts of their doomed relationship, too.

That night, Lauren slept better than she had done for a while. She woke feeling refreshed, and dressed for the continuing warm weather in shorts and her favourite lilac top.

"I think I'll set off for Godlingston House straight after breakfast," she told her mother in the kitchen.

"Fine, love. Only, do take care, won't you?"

Lauren nodded. Just as she was finishing her bowl of cornflakes, the front doorbell rang. Her mother bustled off to answer it.

"There's someone to see you, Lauren," her mother told her, returning to the kitchen. "Do come through, Mr Rossiter."

"Please," a familiar voice replied, "call me Jake."

What was he doing here? Maybe he'd brought a message from the Fergusons, or maybe he'd just dropped in to see her, purely as a friend, of course. Whatever, it looked as though he, too, was having a day off today. He looked casual but good in faded jeans and a navy shirt.

"Hello, Jake," Lauren said, as her heart gave a little involuntary leap. "Jake, this is my mum, Carole," she went on, getting to her feet. "Mum, this is Jake. He's the Fergusons' neighbour, and Mr Ferguson's best friend."

"Pleased to meet you, Carole," Jake said, extending his hand gallantly.

The ringing of the phone cut into their exchange.

"Do excuse me," Carole said. "It's all go in this household."

Seconds after she had answered the

kitchen phone, however, she called over, "Lauren, it's for you."

Lauren, who had been gazing bemusedly at Jake, now murmured her apologies and rushed over to the phone. It was Christine Ferguson.

"Hello, Mrs Ferguson," Lauren said sympathetically. "How are you?"

"Oh, not too bad, thank you. But how are you, Lauren?"

"Oh, I'm fine, thank you, Mrs Ferguson. I spoke to the police yesterday, gave a full statement."

"Well, the thing is," Christine began, "Geoffrey and I have spent some time discussing the situation, and we've decided not to press charges."

"Oh!" Lauren breathed, in surprise. "Neither against Janey nor Stephen?"

"No," Christine agreed. "The police have managed to recover the stolen antiques from local antique shops, not Jake's," she added, with a wry little laugh. "And Janey and Stephen have returned the money. Hopefully that sorry pair have both learned their lesson, and we've stipulated one condition to Janey, that she spends the next two years attending a finishing school in Switzerland. If she still feels the same way about Stephen then, well, we'll see where we go from there."

"I think that's an excellent idea," Lauren said, impressed. "I think you're very brave, Mrs Ferguson," she went on, "the way you've handled all this. I think I would have gone to pieces if it had been me."

"Nonsense," Christine said briskly at the other end of the phone. "Still, it has helped that we've had a bit of good news to cheer us up. Some of Geoffrey's shares suddenly did rather well, and he decided to cash them in and made a huge profit. The long and short of it is, I don't know whether you've heard the rumours flying around about possible staff pay cuts?"

Lauren paused awkwardly.

"Maggie and Derek did mention something to me, yes."

"Well, the good news is that we won't have to cut anyone's pay any more. In fact, we should be able to give everyone a small raise, if you'd still like to work for us, that is."

"Of course I'd still like to work for you."

"Why don't you have a couple of days to think about it?" she suggested generously. "Let me know when you've come to your decision."

"I will do. I'll ring you tomorrow."

But, in her heart of hearts, Lauren already knew that she wanted to return to work for the Fergusons and after she had hung up, she turned back to Jake, who was seated at the kitchen table.

"Strange about the Fergusons deciding not to press charges," she said conversationally.

"I can understand their motives. If it was my own daughter . . ."

They were now alone in the room, her mother having diplomatically made herself scarce.

"So, what can I do for you, Jake?" she asked nicely.

"Oh, there's something I wanted to discuss."

"Actually, I was just going out," she said quickly.

"Oh?" Jake asked, raising a dark eyebrow. "Anywhere nice?"

"Just for a walk," Lauren replied defensively. "To Gorse Hill, as a matter of fact, to look at Godlingston House. Have you heard of it?"

Jake nodded. Seeing him still looking questioningly at her, she gave him a brief, edited version of her great-grandmother's story.

"Poor lady," he said, when she had finished. "It must have been a shock, learning something like that, on top of all this other business."

Lauren shrugged.

"I suppose so. Anyway, that's why I wanted to walk to Gorse Hill, to see the house for myself, try to exorcise the past."

"Mind if I come, too?" Jake asked, taking her by surprise. "It could be an emotional journey, and I'd like to be there for you, in case you need me."

"As a friend," Lauren added with the slightest trace of bitterness.

"Yes, as a friend."

"OK, come if you want to. It's up to you."

"We'll go in my car," Jake said decisively.

"I was rather looking forward to the walk, actually. Still, never mind, I'll come in your car, if you like. Mum!" she called up the stairs, as they were on their way out. "We're off for a walk now! See you later."

Jake parked at his house, then they walked down the hill for a short way, on the lookout for Godlingston House.

"This is it," Jake announced suddenly. "Godlingston House."

It was a square, solid-looking Victorian house. Seeing the tiny servants' windows up in the eaves, Lauren gave a little involuntary shiver. Jake put an arm round her shoulders.

"Yes, thanks," she managed. "It's a bit strange, though, seeing the place where it all happened."

"I'll bet," Jake said sympathetically. "I don't think these people have been here long. I suppose I should pop along one day, introduce myself."

"Turn your legendary charm on them," Lauren said, managing a joke. "Come on. We'd better go. The new owners will think the people of Gorse Hill are all incredibly rude and nosy if we stand here and stare much longer."

They turned round and began to stroll slowly back up the hill.

"Actually," Jake began, "there was a reason why I went to your house to see you today. I was trying to tell you something, the way I feel about you."

"I know. You want us to be just friends."

Jake's expression changed to one of concern.

"Only because I thought that that was what you wanted. Remember the day at the antiques fair, you kept reminding me that we weren't on a date, and we agreed to take it slowly?"

Of course she remembered, Lauren thought bitterly. But she'd been confused then, and unaware of her real feelings.

"But I can't hide my feelings any longer," Jake was saying.

They were just walking past the open gates of Misty Towers, and her attention was drawn to the place she'd come to know so well. Just then the front door was flung open, and Christine appeared with Daniel.

"Lauren, Jake!"

Christine beamed at them. She turned back into the hall.

"Geoffrey! Geoffrey, it's Lauren and Jake! I saw you passing out of the bedroom window. How nice to see you both together," she added.

Geoffrey appeared on the steps. He looked a great deal less stressed than the last time Lauren had seen him. Christine turned to Lauren.

"So," she asked, "will we have to find ourselves a new nanny?"

Lauren smiled at Christine. She couldn't wait to return to Misty Towers.

"No."

"Yes," Jake replied at the same time.

A confused Christine turned from one to the other of them as Jake continued, telling Lauren, "You won't be at work for a while because I want to marry you, Laurie, if you'll have me. And then of course we'll be away on our honeymoon, at least a month, I should think."

"Marry you?" Lauren stuttered. "This is the first I've heard of it."

The corners of Jake's mouth curled in a smile.

"Only because you wouldn't listen. I've been trying to tell you for the last hour and a half."

Jake rummaged in his jacket pocket, producing a black velvet ring-box. He flicked it open to reveal a solitaire diamond engagement ring.

"What a beautiful ring!" Lauren gasped.

"Antique, of course. Edwardian, two carat diamond in a platinum setting with eighteen carat gold band," he said teasingly.

His tone grew serious once again.

"And now I'll ask you properly."

As Christine and Geoffrey melted tactfully away into the house, Jake came closer to her.

"You're so beautiful, Lauren, and you're a lovely, warm, caring person, too. I've been in love with you practically since I first set eyes on you."

Dazedly, Lauren listened to what Jake was saying, hardly daring to believe that it was true. Did he really love her, after all? Had he loved her all this time?

"The only question is," Jake went on, "do you feel the same about me?"

"Oh, yes," Lauren replied unsteadily. "I realised some time ago that I love you, Jake."

"In that case, will you marry me, Lauren?"

"Yes," she replied happily.

Tenderly Jake drew her to him.

"Oh, darling, Laurie, you've no idea how happy you've made me."

Then he kissed her, and Lauren joyfully flung her arms round his neck, kissing him back passionately. There was the sound of applause from the Fergusons' doorway. Pulling guiltily apart, Lauren and Jake saw that Geoffrey and Christine were clapping, even little Daniel was joining in.

"I think this calls for a celebration, Geoffrey," Christine said. "I believe we've got a bottle of champagne in the cellar somewhere, haven't we?"

"How can you think of celebrating at a time like this, my dear?" Geoffrey asked jokingly. "We are going to have to find ourselves a new nanny!"

"Don't worry." Lauren smiled back at her employer. "Seeing as it looks like I'm going to be living next door, hopefully I can still be your nanny."

A pleased-looking Daniel left the safety of his mother's skirts, and ran down the steps to Lauren. He flung himself at her, and she swung the little boy up into her arms.

"Champagne, everyone?" Geoffrey asked, returning with a gold-wrapped green bottle, of which he promptly popped the cork.

He poured the foaming liquid into the champagne flutes Christine was proffering on a silver tray.

"I shouldn't start celebrating yet," Jake warned his friend as he raised his glass. "Lauren might have to be on a fixed-term contract after all."

"Oh?" Geoffrey's brows drew together. "Why's that?"

"Well, she'll only be able to look after Daniel until he goes to school, and after that she'll be too busy looking after our own kids. I expect we'll already have about three by then, and another one on the way!" Jake added with a roguish wink.

"Jake, how presumptuous of you!" Lauren exclaimed, gently swatting her fiancé with her free hand, but she was unable to disguise the joy shining in her eyes and she thought that, just this once, she might forgive him.